Mistletoe Kisses Anthology

Beth Freely, Carol Cassado, Ireland Lorelei, & Patricia Bates

The Book:

This book is a collection of romance short stories over the Christmas holiday. The heat level of the relationships varies between authors.

Each story has a romantic scene under the mistletoe!

A Caribbean Christmas: A St. Pierre Short By Beth A Freely - When a letter from the past is given to twin sister's Branwyn and Igraine St. Pierre, their Christmas celebrations takes an interesting turn. They embark on a treasure hunt like none they've ever taken on before. One that brings the infamous Captain St. Pierre more joy than they bargained for.

An Unforgettable Christmas By Carol Cassada - Taylor and her husband Drew are full of holiday cheer after her family annual Christmas party. However, an accident on the way home as Taylor fighting for her life. A visit from a special guardian angel will make this a Christmas Taylor won't forget.

Mistletoe and Spurs By Patricia Bates – When Holly got her hot cowboy, she knew it was going to be a wild weekend. But secrets have a way of coming out and to get her happily ever after, they will need a little more mistletoe magic.

Trapped in a Blizzard By Ireland Lorelei – Perla is on her way to a ski resort and her car breaks down in the middle of a blizzard. Troy is a police officer on vacation in his cabin over the holidays. He rescues Perla and gets more than he bargained for!

The Author:

Beth Freely, Carol Cassado, Ireland Lorelei, & Patricia Bates

Mistletoe Kisses Anthology

by

Beth Freely, Carol Cassado, Ireland Lorelei, & Patricia Bates

Warrioress Publishing - Jacksonville, FL

1. Edition, 2022

© 2022 All rights reserved.

Warrioress Publishing - Jacksonville, FL

Table of Contents

A Caribbean Christmas   1

An Unforgettable Christmas   35

Mistletoe and Spurs 70

Trapped in a Blizzard   149

A Caribbean Christmas

By Beth A. Freely

Chapter One

Somewhere in the Caribbean, 1726, December 20

"Fletcher!"

Captain Ayden Fletcher flinched at the bellow that came from the hold of the merchant vessel, *Fortune's Wind*. He briefly looked up at the crow's nest, a smile crossing his tanned face. His hands deftly turned the ship's wheel, making minor adjustments as the wind filled the sails.

"Fletcher!" the voice called again.

Beth Freely, Carol Cassado, Ireland Lorelei, & Patricia

The notes of frustration were enough to make him sigh. He looked to his boatswain and turned the wheel of the ship over to him. He calmly walked to the stairs as the ship pitched and rolled on the waves. A storm was brewing, in the heaven's above and on the deck below. "Wyn, what has you in such a state?" He stood at the top step, gazing down at the woman emerging from the hold. Branwyn St. Pierre still took his breath away, the same way she did when she first walked into the Pirate's Quarry on Tobago and aimed a loaded pistol at his head.

"Are ye even listening to me, Fletcher?" she asked. He had a stupid grin on his face as he gazed down at her. She knew that grin. That grin meant trouble and her on her back in their bed. She felt her cheeks warm. "Ayden." His grin grew a bit. Branwyn sighed at pulled the dagger from her boot. She threw it towards him, the tip burying itself in the wood of the railing next to his head.

"Bloody hell, lamb! What was that for?"

Branwyn folded her arms over her chest. "Because I was trying to talk to you. But you were staring at me like I was one of your streetside doxies and that grin of yours was starting to anger me."

Ayden pulled her dagger free and slowly made his way down the steps to the main deck. He handed her the blade hilt first. "First off, lamb, you put to shame any streetside doxy I ever parlayed with," he said quietly. He cupped her face in the rough palm of his hand. "And I like it when you get angry," he finished, his lips capturing hers in a kiss that made the crew hoot and holler. He leaned back, smiling. "Now, what has you in this right snit?"

Branwyn took a step back from him. She needed to think, and he was very good at making her forget everything when he kissed her. She held up her hands, still holding her dagger. "What has me in this right snit is that I just checked the cargo and we be missing two cases of rum. I know we had them when we left Barbados but now they be gone."

"They're not gone, lamb."

She shook her head. "I may not be much for reading, Fletcher, but I can count, and I can keep a ledger. We be two cases shy."

Ayden chuckled. "Wyn, the two cases are in our cabin. Your sister ordered them for the family. For the Christmas party she is hosting on Christmas Eve. The one you promised we'd be home for."

Branwyn's eyes narrowed. She remembered her sister talking about a big to-do at the St. Pierre estate for the holidays. A party like hadn't been seen since their parents were alive. She cursed under her breath. "Bloody hell."

"The bolts of fabric you picked out are also there. And I will guarantee that she will have you standing in front of a seamstress the moment you set foot in the house." He nodded towards the horizon. The island of Martinique was just visible, its dark shape looming in the distance like a specter. He leaned toward her, whispering in her ear, "But we have plenty of time before we arrive. And I'm sure Mr. Twain can handle her until then. Aye?"

Branwyn raised one dark eyebrow at him, before following his gaze. "What's the chance of getting out of the holiday celebrations and sneaking off to Tobago to celebrate on our own?" she countered.

"Slim, I would say. You know they will be waiting for us at the dock. And if I know Mako, he's already on the widow's walk with the spyglass in hand to see if we are close."

"Can we swap flags?" she asked. "I'm sure we still have a Jolly Roger somewhere." Her lips twitched in amusement at the suggestion. After all, they hadn't always been honest sailors. She was Captain St. Pierre, the pirate that could be in two places at one time and he was "Bloody Cutlass" Fletcher, the notorious rogue of the seven seas.

"Wyn," Ayden chuckled.

"It was a thought!" she protested.

Ayden pulled her into his arms, her back to his chest as they stood on the deck of the *Fortune's Wind* and watched their home come closer. "Do you really want to disappoint Igraine like that? You know she longs for you to stay at the estate longer than we do."

"Aye, I know she does." She leaned back against Ayden, folding her hands over his at her waist. They fell into an easy silence as the ship rode the waves. She closed her eyes, feeling the wind on her face and relaxed. "Maybe this time we can stay longer. Or at least try."

"Until the sea calls us back."

"Aye. Until the sea calls us back." She

turned in his arms, breaking the embrace. The storm chasing them filled their sails, giving them a push toward shore. "Do ye still think Mr. Twain can handle her and get us into port?"

Ayden followed her gaze. They would reach the estate before the storm hit the island. He nodded. "Aye, I do."

"Then what did you have in mind and is our bunk involved?" She met his brown eyed gaze. "I could use a rest. Bolster up me courage to face me sister's army of seamstresses and shoemakers."

"Aye, our bunk is involved. And you can rest for as long as you want, lamb." Ayden ran a finger down her cheek to her neck before tracing the line of her collarbone just visible above her blouse.

"Mr. Twain! Bring her into port. Captain Fletcher and I have some things to discuss below," Branwyn called, pulling Ayden with her to their cabin.

Chapter Two

The door to Branwyn's bedroom in the St. Pierre manor burst open as Igraine St. Pierre marched in. She was going to sweep her twin up in a sisterly hug but stopped short at the sight of Branwyn's naked rear end poking out of the tub. Apparently her sister had dropped something over the side of the large wooden bath and was trying to reach it without getting out of the steaming water. Igraine's eyes traced down her sister's back. Her heart ached knowing that many of the whip mark scars Branwyn carried were on her behalf.

"Oh, bloody hell," Branwyn murmured. She stood, her long hair falling down her back and hiding the whip marks. She reached out and grabbed her sword, using the tip of it to capture the errant tankard by its handle. "Ha!" she exclaimed. She slipped it off her sword and turned to the table behind her. "Igraine! When did ye get home?" She grinned at her sister, refilling her tankard from the pitcher, and settling back down in the hot water. "I half expected you and Mako at the docks to greet us."

Igraine folded her arms over her chest and tried to glower sternly at the other woman. But the smile on Branwyn's face was infectious and she chuckled, shaking her head as she walked to the edge of the tub. Her brow furrowed at the sight of another tankard sitting there and she peered into the tub, half expecting to see Ayden hiding under the water. "Well, we planned on it, but the storm came in so fast we were caught at dinner with the head of the merchant's guild." She looked around the room as lightning lit the sky. "I take it this is Fletcher's tankard?" she inquired.

Branwyn snorted. "Yours now. Since you're home, he'll be talking with Mako half the night." She moved through the water and waited until Igraine filled her tankard before tapping her own against it. "Cheers, mate."

They both drank, Branwyn wiping the ale from her lips with the back of her hand while Igraine sipped hers daintily. She pointed to the pile of paper wrapped items on the bed. "Now, before you think about calling any of your fancy seamstresses here to the manor, we need to have a long conversation about the type of dress I'll be wearing to this to-do of yours."

Igraine's eyes followed Branwyn's arm, and she set the tankard down. "I'm excited yet scared to see what you brought, Branwyn."

"Oy, I got what you asked for," Branwyn protested.

Igraine raised an eyebrow at her sister's protest. She saw the dagger lying with Branwyn's clothing and picked it up, cutting through the strings that held the package together. "There is a new seamstress on the island that will come and make our dresses. She insists she and her girls can have them ready in time for the party. She's already finished all the petticoats and undergarments. And I already informed her that you have an aversion to corsets and stays."

"Aye, I do."

Igraine peeled back the paper and gasped in pleasant surprise. "Oh, Branwyn," she whispered. She looked at her twin. They were as different as night and day when it came to everything but their looks. Identical twins, Branwyn was bold and brash, a child of the sea and as wild as the men that sailed under her. Igraine was refined, well-educated and a true lady of the manor. "Where did you find these?"

The silk bolts in the packages were of deep green and burgundy, perfect for holiday garments. The green silk was striped in complimenting green and gold, while the burgundy carried a cream lace pattern interspersed with what looked like mistletoe flowers. There was less of the burgundy and Igraine knew that Branwyn had picked that for herself. Burgundy always did look better on her.

"This tiny little shop in Boston." Branwyn turned to the window, watching as the storm continued out toward the sea, having dumped its rain and cool air on Martinique. "It's the only thing Hammond ever gave me that was worthwhile, a report with the owner." She hated speaking of their former guardian, and she shivered slightly. She took a deep breath and turned back to Igraine. "Anyway, there is enough for us each to have a dress and for Fletcher and Mako new waistcoats."

Igraine heard the hitch in her sister's voice as she mentioned Hammond but paid it no mind. It would not do to dwell on the horrible memories of him. She looked at the rest of the packages. "What is all this then?"

Branwyn shrugged. "Well, I could use some new shirts and britches on the ship, and I thought you could use some new dresses, seeing as you're the lady of the manor. So, I splurged a bit." She grabbed the towel from the bed and wrapped it around her body as she stepped out of the tub. She took the dagger from Igraine and sliced the twine on the rest of the packages. "Ayden and I ran into Abigail and Johnny Devereaux while we were there. Abigail helped me choose some of these for you." She winked as she sheathed her dagger and made her way to her wardrobe. She pulled on her robe, letting the towel drop to the floor.

"*Mon deux*, did you splurge," Igraine laughed as she looked at the bolts of rich and vibrant fabric her sister had brought home.

Branwyn plopped down at the head of her bed, an apple in hand. She took a bite. "So, who is coming to this party of yours and what kind of food are we having? Is it like the parties Pa used to have?"

Igraine nodded. "Of course. The crews of the *Fortune's Wind* and the *Golden Ranger* will be there.. and…"

"Wait. The *Golden Ranger*?" Branwyn stared at her sister.

"Surprise."

"We have a second ship?" Branwyn was sitting on her knees at her sister's proclamation.

"We do."

"And it's the *Golden Ranger*? Who be captainin' it?"

Igraine laughed. "We don't have a captain for it yet, which is what I suspect Ayden and Mako are discussing. Mako mentioned offering it to Shamus or Mr. Twain." She paused. "Unless you want it."

Branwyn's eyes went wide as she thought about it. To be the sole captain of a ship…even when she was the captain of the *Sassenach's Bane* sailing for Hammond she was not the only captain. She shared that title with Igraine even though her twin never took control of the ship while out on the open water. And there was always someone there watching her, waiting to take over if she slipped up. But as much as the thought of having her own ship appealed to her, she had found everything that she ever longed for in Ayden Fletcher. The thought of being away from him for months at a time made her shake her head. "No. No, I be happy sailing with Fletcher. But Twain would be a good captain. And Shamus a good first mate." She leaned back on the bed, grinning. "We got us a fleet."

Igraine nodded. "*Oui*. We do."

Chapter Three

Three days before Christmas

"Ow, you bloody twit! Do ye not know where your pins be going?" Branwyn snapped. She looked at the young woman pinning fabric in place around her midriff. "That be the sixth time you stabbed me. I not be some witch's poppet!"

The seamstress, a woman named Estella, approached Branwyn. She took the pins from her assistant, said something to the younger woman in Italian and sent her to do something else. "You must forgive her, Lady Branwyn. Her skills at needlework far surpass her skills at pinning."

"And her hands were bloody cold!" Branwyn added, noticing how warm Estrella's hands were. She was tired of standing there with her arms out, like she was the mast of her ship. She watched as Estrella finished pinning the burgundy fabric without poking her once. "You're not…you're not planning on putting stays in this bloody dress, are ye?"

"No. I have other ways of making your dress work to uplift and fill. You are not the first lady who despises the limitations of corsets and stays." She pointed to Branwyn. "There. Let us get you out of this." She helped Branwyn ease from the dress without getting poked by the pins in the fabric.

The door to the dressing room opened and Igraine stepped in. "Excuse me. Branwyn, we have a visitor asking to speak with us both." She folded her hands at her waist and waited.

"Aye? Who?"

"Christoph Bingham."

"Bingham? Why is he bloody here?" Branwyn grabbed her pants and pulled them on before slipping off the petticoats. She pulled her shirt over her head and slipped on her vest, buttoning it as she followed her sister from the room. "We did nothing wrong!"

"Nobody said you did," Igraine stated. Bingham was known as a pirate hunter even though most of the notorious ones had been captured or pardoned already. She looked down at the sound of her twin's feet slapping the marble. "You aren't wearing any shoes, sister," Igraine pointed out, trying not to smile.

Branwyn shrugged. "The cool floor feels good on me feet," she mumbled. It was true. The marble of the manor floor was smooth, a stark contrast to the rough-hewn boards that made up the deck of the *Fortune's Wind*. She paused for a moment to watch one of their staff as they draped evergreen garland over the side of the balcony. A large fir tree was being placed in the foyer, the only place large enough to accommodate it. "Is it big enough?" Branwyn asked as she hurried down the stairs after her sister.

Bingham heard Branwyn's question and chuckled. "With a foyer this large, one can only expect a tree this big." He bowed slightly to the sisters. "I remember your father having trees this big as well. I'm sure Fletcher does too." He took

Igraine's hand, kissing the back of it. "Igraine." He sent a snarky wink in Branwyn's direction. "Captain."

"Bingham," Branwyn replied. "You come to clap me in irons or is this a friendly visit?"

Bingham laughed. "A friendly visit." He reached into his vest and pulled out a parchment sealed with red wax. "I was asked to deliver this to both of you when the time was right. It was the last task your father gave me before he passed." He handed the letter to Igraine.

Igraine looked at the letter. "Do you know what this contains?"

"Part of it as Captain St. Pierre had a task for me that pertained to it." Bingham held up his hands. "You'll understand. I am just the messenger." He grinned. "I am looking forward to the party. And I promise, my crew will be on their best behavior." He picked up his hat, touched his fingers to it in salute to the sisters and strode through the front door.

Branwyn looked at the parchment in her sister's hands. "What is that, then?"

Igraine shook her head. "It looks like a letter." She turned and walked into the sitting room. The day was warm, and Louis, their butler, had opened the windows, letting the sea breeze blow through the room. She sat down in one of the armchairs and opened the letter. Branwyn paced by the open window, enjoying the breeze on her face. Igraine read the letter aloud.

1708

My sweetest Igraine and my wild Wyn,
I fear that I will not make it home for our Christmas celebration. The seas are not in my favor this year and Hammond has had me and the lads sailing from the colonies and back at every turn.

In lieu of our annual party, I have arranged for something just as fun for my beauties. Attached to this letter is a map. I have hidden two gifts somewhere on the estate, one for my Igraine and one for my Wyn. Together, I want you to read that map and discover my gifts. I know you can find what I have left behind.

I love you both and I cannot wait to hear about your adventure.
With love and adoration,
Papa

Branwyn looked at her sister. "Papa left a map?"

Igraine opened the second piece of parchment and began to laugh. "Well, if you can call it a map."

Branwyn looked at the map her sister held up and started to laugh. "Aye, it's a map. But an easy one to follow."

"We're following a map?" Ayden asked as he walked into the sitting room, Mako Jon behind him.

"Aye. Our father left us…well…treasure," Branwyn replied. She noticed the mistletoe hanging in the doorway, and she walked towards Ayden. "He set up a treasure hunt and hid some presents for us." She slipped her arms around his waist. "You know I love looking for treasure." She glanced up at him, leaning in to steal a kiss.

"A treasure, aye?" He gently pushed Branwyn aside and walked over to Igraine and the map. He was well aware of the mistletoe hanging above him, but he was going to make his lover work for the kiss. "Well, you are a pirate, lamb," he called back.

Branwyn nodded. "Aye, and ye best not be forgetting that, Fletcher." She turned back to her sister and the men. "Why you still sitting there? We have treasure to be finding and I think we waited long enough."

Chapter Four

Branwyn paused in her search for her father's gifts long enough to pull on her boots and sneak a piece of mistletoe out of Louis' Christmas decorations. She was going to get that scallywag Fletcher to give her a kiss under it one way or another. After studying the map their father had left her, she had a good idea of where he left their gifts. But she didn't tell Igraine. Her sister's joy was infectious, and Branwyn knew she loved a good puzzle.

They decided to split up. Branwyn was headed to the barn where she was sure one of the gifts was located. There were two 'Xs' on the map, one in the house and one outside. When her father made the map, the barn was only a small outbuilding with the larger structure being completed long after he had been murdered by their guardian, Hammond. It was to the small outbuilding she was headed.

"Lamb, wait up!"

"Not now, Fletcher!" she called as she marched into the barn and stopped. She blinked in the cool darkness of the building, letting her eyes adjust. The small outbuilding had become the tack room once the barn was finished, and she was sure she would quickly find the gift. She was about to continue towards it when a set of strong arms wrapped around her waist and lifted her to her feet. "Fletcher! Put me down!" she laughed.

"No, lamb. Not until you tell me what led you out here." He carried her deeper into the barn, looking in each stall until he found one with an ample amount of fresh, clean hay. He looked around for a moment before dumping her into the pile. He closed the stall door.

Branwyn looked up at her lover. "What are ye playing at, Fletcher?" she asked.

Straw was stuck in her long hair and her braid was disheveled. He was about to dishevel so much more. "You said we were looking for treasure. You know how I like a good treasure hunt. You do remember what happened the last time, don't you lamb?" he whispered low as he untied his pants.

Branwyn's face grew heated in memory. "Aye, you ruined one of my best shirts," she teased, working at the ties of her own pants. Ayden grabbed one foot and tugged her boot off before yanking her pants down, making her squeal. "I've got straw poking me bum," she laughed as he sank to his knees before her, pulling her to him.

"That's not the only thing about to poke you, lamb," he growled before impaling her on his hardened shaft. His mouth captured hers as she sat up and wrapped her legs around him with a deep moan. She was hot and tight and ready for him, her body wrapping around his like a warm cocoon.

"I much prefer you poking me, Fletcher," she gasped when he ended the kiss. She worked the buttons of her vest open and felt his hand slip under her shirt to cup her breast. His mouth trailed down her neck as she rode him. She gripped his upper arms as they moved together, the thought of her father's gift temporarily gone from her mind. Ayden Fletcher had a habit of making her forget things. She groaned as he quickened his pace, his mouth capturing hers again in a fervent kiss.

It wasn't long before their passions were spent, and they lay in the hay pile sated, slowly coming down from the euphoria they had shared. Branwyn had her head on his shoulder and smiled as he traced circles on her back. The sounds of the barn surrounded them, the scent of the hay and the horses in the stalls across the way almost as soothing as the rise and fall of a ship at sea. Fletcher made her feel safe and loved.

Branwyn didn't know how long she dozed, but soft cry of an animal brought her around. She listened for a moment, unsure if she had dreamed it or if somewhere in the barn an animal was in distress. She heard it again and nudged Ayden in the ribs as she sat up. "Do ye hear that?"

"Hear what?" Ayden asked sleepily.

"That cry," she replied. She slipped her foot into her pants leg and stood, quickly fastening them before pulling on her boot. She grabbed her vest and looked around, realizing that the piece of mistletoe she had pilfered from Louis' pile was nowhere to be found. She heard the cry again and forgot the piece of Christmas greenery. She opened the stall door and looked around as she slipped on her vest and buttoned it. "It's coming from the tack room."

"What is, lamb?" Ayden called.

"That cry." She turned and looked at him, spying the mistletoe lying on the ground by his foot. Quickly, she marched over to him, scooped up the plant and kicked the bottom of his boot. "C'mon Fletcher." She didn't wait for him. She left the stall and headed to the tack room, yanking the door open.

The tack room was dark, only a small window at the top of the room lighting it. The light didn't reach the floor. Branwyn listened for a moment and then jumped as something brushed against her.

"Mew."

Branwyn looked down at the small cry. Twisting around her ankles was a small orange tabby kitten wearing a big red Christmas bow. She picked the kitten up. "Well, where did you come from?" she asked it.

"It has a tag on it's bow. An old tag by the looks of it," Ayden commented behind her. He reached around her and read it. "*To Igraine. May this kitten always be a source of comfort and enjoyment when your sister is not around. Love, Papa.*" He scratched the kitten behind its ears. "You found your sister's gift. So that means…"

"She's on the hunt of the gift Papa left for me." Branwyn lifted the kitten up to her face and rubbed her cheek in its soft fur. The little animal started purring and licked her nose. She turned him around and chuckled before cuddling him close. "A lady killer then," she exclaimed as she carried the little animal from the barn. "Let's go see if my sister has found my gift yet. Depending on what it is will help me decide whether or not I want to give this little guy up."

Chapter Five

Igraine gazed at the map as she and Mako Jon wandered through the manor house. She clenched the map tightly. She didn't want to lose it as it was a small part of their father that they would always treasure. She wondered how her sister was doing in her own treasure hunt. "I have no idea what Papa would've left us. He's never done… never did anything like this before." She clasped Mako Jon's hand. "This is exciting, *mon cherie*."

Mako Jon smiled. "I wonder why Bingham only brought your father's letter to you now," he pondered aloud.

"Maybe he was not in the islands last Christmas," Igraine countered. She started down the stone steps that led to the kitchen below. "Or he forgot about it."

Mako nodded. "Maybe." More than likely, the former pirate hunter didn't feel the time was quite right. The sister's had only just won their freedom from their guardian Hammond, and Branwyn and Ayden cleared of all charges of piracy. Their Christmas the previous year had been just the four of them, quiet and intimate.

The kitchen was bustling when they entered, the St. Pierre staff preparing countless baked goods for the celebration. Igraine smiled at Francois and approached him with her map, asking him in his native French if he knew the location marked with an 'X.' Mako looked around, not paying attention to the conversation. Instead, he snuck one of the pastries on the counter before him, holding his finger up to his lips when one of the kitchen girls saw him sneak a taste. He smiled at her, and she smiled back in silent conspiracy.

"Jon, it is over here," Igraine called.

Mako Jon picked up another pastry, popping it in his mouth as he joined his fiancée. He looked at the large cabinet she was pointing at. "Exactly where, my love?"

Igraine pointed up. "Francois said he remembers when my father put the gift up there. He claims that Papa said the one who finds this gift will have to be creative to get it down." She watched as Mako reached to the top of the cabinet. "Well?"

"There is something up here. I'm just trying to get my fingers around it," he grunted. He finally managed to grab a hold of something solid and pulled it down. It was wrapped in plain paper, and it held a bit of weight.

"I will open it in the drawing room," Igraine said. She thanked Francois and the kitchen staff for their help as she made her way back upstairs. By the time she entered the drawing room, Branwyn and Ayden were already there. "Did you find the gift?"

"Aye. Did you?" Branwyn asked.

"I did." She joined her sister and Ayden before the fire. "Well, let's open them."

"The one I found was already open," Branwyn stated as she picked up the soft pillow the orange kitten was sleeping on. "Apparently this little boy was for you." She handed Igraine the tag she had removed from the kitten's ribbon.

Igraine cooed for a moment at the cat, gently petting its tiny head. "How precious." She looked at Branwyn. "But how can he be from Papa? Wouldn't he have grown?"

It was an interesting question and Branwyn scratched her head. "I suspect Bingham has an answer to that." She nodded to the package Igraine had laid on the table. "What did you find?"

"It's your present. You open it."

"No. You found it. You open it," Branwyn insisted.

Igraine shrugged. She carefully untied the ribbon that held the paper together and peeled it free from the gift. Inside was a kukri dagger, the exact mate to the one Branwyn carried. She looked at the small letter left inside. "*To me wild Wyn, You have proven a master with the dagger I already gave you. Here is its mate. Use them only in self-defense or whenever a task requires something more than a simple knife. Do not let your mother know you have these. I love you always. Papa.*" Igraine pulled the curved dagger free from its sheath, the sunlight glinting on the blade. "This definitely belongs to you."

Branwyn had been petting the kitten and she looked up to her sister. "No. No this time, that blade be yours." She stood up and walked over to Igraine. "It's the twin to mine and you're my twin. It only makes sense that you carry that."

Igraine met Branwyn's gaze. It wasn't often that she displayed that kind of sweet sentiment. "If it means that much to you, then I will keep it." She looked at the kitten. "Have you thought of a name for him?"

Branwyn looked back at the sleeping pile of fluff. "I think I'll call him Fletcher."

"Say what?" Ayden asked looking up at her.

Branwyn scooped the kitten up with one hand, cuddling it close. "Aye. Fletcher." She walked to the doorway, stopping under the mistletoe, waiting for him.

"And why would you bloody well name him that?" Ayden said as he walked towards her.

"Because then ye'll never know if I'm yelling at him or you." She grinned.

"That's cold, lamb. That's cold." He looked up at the mistletoe and slipped past her. "Mako! Care to nip on down to the tavern and check on the boys with me?" He smiled at Branwyn, pointing up to the mistletoe with a wink before turning on one foot and marching from the house, leaving Branwyn staring at him.

"Oh, you're going to kiss me, Ayden Fletcher," she whispered. "One way or another, you're going to kiss me."

Chapter Six

Christmas Eve

Igraine smiled at her guests as she moved through the ballroom on Mako Jon's arm. She was making sure that all of her guests were well taken care of. The decorations were perfect, the small quartet playing in the corner was in tune and the crews from the three ships – the *Fortune's Wind*, the *Golden Ranger,* and Christoph Bingham's ship – were acting like proper gentlemen.

The only thing missing was Branwyn. Igraine was not surprised her sister had not yet made an appearance at the party. The party was not her type of gathering. She sighed, looking toward Ayden, Mako Jon and Bingham. She made her way to the three men.

"Ah, there you are," Mako greeted, taking her hand, and raising it to her lips. "You look stunning, *mon cherie*." The green silk of her dress shined in the candlelight that filled the room. He leaned in to whisper, "I will enjoy ravishing you later."

Igraine squeezed his hand as she looked to the other men. "Branwyn?" she asked Ayden.

"She's still getting ready. She is not happy with her hair or her shoes or her dress…petticoats…stockings…" Ayden shrugged and sipped at the drink in his hand. "Which reminds me. Bingham here has an interesting story about the kitten."

"Oh? Do tell," Igraine encouraged.

"Well, when I arrived here with your father's body, I took the time to seek out the original kitten he had acquired for you. It was being taken care of by one of the stable hands. It was a female, so I took her with me, and she sailed with me and my crew for years. One of the old toms below deck put her in the family way," Bingham chuckled. "I kept one of the offspring. I've done that with every batch of kittens, always keeping one on board the ship that was a direct descendant of the original kitten your father meant for you."

"And the other kittens?" Igraine asked.

"They are running around my estate back in New England. They are excellent mousers," Bingham laughed.

The music changed to a lively dance and Mako Jon looked at Igraine. "Shall we, milady?"

Ayden watched as Mako Jon swept her into his arms and across the dance floor. Bingham took his leave, wandering over to a cluster of his crew and joining their conversation. He was about to go and refill his tankard with punch when he saw her standing in the doorway. Branwyn St. Pierre looked magnificent in the burgundy gown. Her hair was swept up in intricate curls atop her head and a beautiful pendant of sapphire graced her neck. He felt his body tighten at the sight of her, his pulse quickening. Her eyes darted around the room until they landed on him, and he watched her nervousness disappear. He set his tankard down and made his way through the crowd to her. He stopped before her, simply admiring the way she looked in the gown.

"What are ye staring at, Fletcher?" she asked softly. The way he was looking at her made her blush and she hated to blush. "Stop it," she hissed.

Ayden stepped closer to her, blocking her view of the party. "I am looking at the most beautiful woman in all of the Caribbean." He took her hands in his, raising them to his lips. "Never before have I set my eyes on a more exquisite creature. You are my heart and soul, Branwyn St. Pierre. And I would go to the ends of the earth for you."

"I think ye might already have," she teased him. She gazed up at him. His brown eyes were dark with need but also filled with more love and devotion than she was used to seeing. "Your namesake might have claimed ye pillow," she whispered.

"So, the name Fletcher is sticking then," Ayden groaned softly, tugging her closer to him.

"Oh aye, the name is sticking and he's going to have run of our cabin on the *Fortune's Wind*."

"Is he now?"

"Aye."

Ayden slipped his arm around her waist, pulling her against him. The silk of the dress was soft beneath his palm. "Well then, we may have to set up his own little bunk. I'm not sure ours could handle another sleeping in it." He glanced up to the mistletoe above her head and then back to her, a smile tilting his lips. "Merry Christmas, Branwyn," he whispered before lowering his mouth to hers in a searing kiss filled with promise, love, and devotion.

Beth Freely, Carol Cassado, Ireland Lorelei, & Patricia

The End

An Unforgettable Christmas

By Carol Cassada

Bing Crosby's voice filled the air while children squealed with delight with their new dolls and monster trucks. Colorful nights decorated the tree while balls of wrapping paper scattered underneath the artificial greenery. The men gathered in the living room to discuss sports while the women put up the leftovers.

Taylor smiled while wrapping aluminum foil around a plate of pigs in a blanket. Meanwhile, her mother Susan and sisters-in-law Mallory and Gina complained about doing all the work while the men goofed off.

Taylor shook her head at the complaints, Christmas wasn't the time to be grumpy. It's about cheer, love, and family. Taylor was somewhat of a holiday aficionado and Christmas was her favorite time of year. She loved everything from decorating to baking to buying gifts. But most importantly she loved being with her family.

There'd been plenty of memorable Christmas for Taylor. When she was eight she remembered jumping for joy when Santa brought her a Barbie dream house. Then there was the family ski trip when she was fourteen, the first time she'd ever went away for Christmas. But her favorite Christmas moment came two years ago.

Taylor was already in a joyous mood as she woke up to make breakfast for her and her boyfriend Drew. After scarfing down a stack of chocolate chip pancakes, they retreated to the living room to open gifts.

Taylor noticed Drew was acting odd, a bit nervous. "What should we open first?" She looked at the gifts stacked neatly around the tree.

"I see a special gift for a special lady." Drew reached behind the tree to pull out a blue wrapped box.

Taylor arched her eyebrow at the box, she hadn't noticed it when she put the presents out yesterday. But Drew was a master when it came to hiding gifts. He probably put it there when she wasn't looking.

She took the box from Drew and shook it. It made a rattle which piqued her curiosity.

"Open it." Drew smiled as he watched Taylor tear into the gift like a kid.

Taylor tossed the paper aside to find a white and red striped box. She opened it and unraveled the green tissue paper to find a trinket box ornament. The red ball was decorated with poinsettias with the inscription joy to the world.

"Drew, it's so pretty. It'll look good on the tree."

"Hold on, there's more." He pointed to the ornament. "Look inside."

Taylor careful opened the trinket and her mouth dropped open at the sight of the heart shaped diamond ring. When she glanced at Drew, he was on bended knee.

"Taylor, I never thought I'd find a woman as beautiful and kind-hearted as you. From the moment we met, you captured my heart. Now I want you to hold onto it forever. Will you marry me?"

"Yes," Taylor screamed before jumping into Drew's arms.

"The men are still talking about football." Mallory grumbled as she carried empty plastic cups into the kitchen.

"That's all they ever do," Susan replied as she put lids on the cans of ranch and cheddar dips.

"All except Drew," Gina piped in. "Taylor you got a real man there."

Taylor smiled at the compliment. She wasn't one to brag about her husband, but she admitted she hit the jackpot with him. Although Drew loved football as much as any guy, he wasn't as passionate about it as some were.

"Speaking of, I better go find him. We have to leave in a few." Taylor excused herself and exited the kitchen. She glanced into the living room to see her dad and brothers engaged in an animated conversation. Her nieces and nephew were curled on the sofa watching A Charlie Brown Christmas.

Taylor then walked down the hall and peeked into the den to see Drew playing checkers with Grandpa William. The older man scratched his white beard, then rubbed his bald head as he contemplated his next move. After a second he moved his red checker into a corner.

Drew's hand hovered over the board trying to figure out how to win the game with one checker left. William was ganging up on him and he needed an exit plan. He moved his checker to the right, only after he placed it in the box did he realize his mistake. William had him trapped from both sides and with a double checker jumped Drew's piece.

"Better luck next time, Drew." William held out his hand and Drew shook it in defeat.

"I'll practice for our next rematch." Out of the hundreds of times they played, William's win record was higher than Drew's. "Can I get you anymore eggnog?"

"No thanks, I've had enough for tonight."

Drew took their empty cups and headed for the doorway where he met his wife. "Your grandpa is a tough competitor."

"He's always has a strong personality." Taylor's smile faltered as she thought about the grief her family went through earlier this year.

In September , William's beloved wife and Taylor's grandmother Grace passed away. Grace's death was unexpected, the day before she was cheery as the family gathered for a Labor Day barbecue. Grace's energy was in full swing as she made her famous potato salad then later participated in the horseshoe toss.

Little did Taylor and the rest of the family know that was the last time they'd see Grace alive.

The next morning William awoke and went downstairs, expecting to see Grace sitting in the kitchen having her cereal and coffee. Instead he found her slumped on the sofa, dead of a heart attack.

Taylor would never forget her mother calling to break the grim news. She went through all the stages of grief during the phone conversation. Taylor knew eventually the time would come, Grace was pushing eighty, but she hoped to have more time with her grandmother.

Grace's death hit William the hardest. Although he put on a brave front, deep down Taylor knew he was hurting. They were together for fifty-seven years, a rarity in today's world. Yet, their love and devotion to each other never wavered.

Taylor hoped she and Drew could have a love like that.

"Are you thinking about your grandmother?" Drew's rugged voice broke her thoughts.

Taylor nodded, fearing if she spoke she'd break down.

"It's okay." Drew shifted the cups to his other hand to give Taylor a side hug. "It's always difficult, but the holidays is when it hits you the most."

"You got that right." Taylor glanced at William, who was putting the checkers in the box. "How's he doing? Has he mentioned…"

Drew shook his head. "He hasn't talked about her, but every now and then I caught him looking at her photo."

"I'm going to go check on him."

"Hold on." Pulled her back into his arms and his gaze shifted to the mistletoe hanging above the doorway. He leaned down and planted a kiss on her red lips. "Couldn't let you get out of the mistletoe tradition"

"There will be plenty more tonight," Taylor giggled as she watched her husband disappear into the kitchen. She then entered the den and sat in the chair vacated by Drew.

"I love that husband of yours, but he's no good at checkers."

"Poker and Monopoly are more his games."

William looked up to make sure Drew wasn't around then leaned closer to Taylor. "Sometimes I think he lets me win."

"You May have a point," Taylor laughed.

"Grace used to do the same thing. She was a pro at checkers, but she'd throw a game to make me feel better." William pursed his lips as his eyes moved to a framed photo on the table. The picture was taken during William and Grace's fifty-fifth anniversary party. Grace looked charming in a pale pink dress, with her short white hair curled to perfection, while William was dapper in a navy blue suit. The couple's joy shined in their expressions as they cut the angel food cake while surrounded by family and friends.

"How are you feeling, grandpa?"

"I'd be lying if I said I was alright." William's fingers brushed the gold frame. "There are days where I'm fine, but there are times like today where I miss her."

William remembered how Grace always was cheerful around Christmas just like Taylor. He joked that Taylor inherited her grandmother's love of the holiday. Every year, Grace made sure the house was filled with Christmas joy with her colorful sparkly decorations and homemade food.

"I wasn't sure if I was up to celebrating this year. But then I thought about what Grace would do. She say, 'William, get out of your slump and enjoy the Christmas festivities.'"

Taylor laughed at William's impersonation of Grace's shrill voice. "That sounds like something she'd do."

"I like to think she's looking down at us, smiling that the family is together."

Taylor solemnly nodded. If there was a thing as guardian angels, she believed Grace was one. Even when she was on Earth, she was looking after everyone, providing love and comfort.

"I was blessed to have her. Even though we had our difficult times, we stuck with each other through thick and thin. Whenever I had a bad day, just her smile and positive attitude was enough change my tune."

"That's beautiful."

William nodded. "I see a lot of myself and Grace in you and Drew. The way you two look at each other as if you're the only two people in the room, that's how me and Grace were."

"I hope we're as lucky to have fifty-seven years together." Taylor glanced into the doorway to see Drew talking with Susan who was offering him leftovers to take home.

"You're well on your way. Just remember to cherish every moment you have together."

The party winded down and all of the family left William's house, except Taylor and Drew. They stayed behind to make sure everything was locked up and the house was clean.

William shook his head as he watched Drew double-checking to make sure the tree was unplugged while Taylor wiped a water ring from the end table.

"You two kids don't have to do all that," William ordered.

"We want to make sure we didn't forget anything, we worry about you grandpa."

Although Taylor and Drew lived ten minutes from William, she worried about him now that he was alone. She made it a priority to call him every day, and three times a week she and Drew stopped by to check on him.

"I'm fine, although I'll be better once I can go to bed."

Taylor giggled knowing they were keeping him up with their antics. "Sorry, grandpa. We'll be going now." She gave a peck on the cheek. "Thanks for a lovely time."

"I should be thanking you and your mother, you did all the work."

"I wanted to make grandma proud."

"You did." He patted Taylor's head. "She would've loved this."

Drew came into the foyer carrying his and Taylor's coats. "William, it was fun as always."

"Glad you enjoy yourself." He hugged his grandson-in-law. "Remember, to practice at checkers. I'm getting tired of humiliating you every game."

"This weekend, you and I have a rematch."

"Sounds good." William and Drew shook hands to seal the deal. "Now, you two get going or else Santa may skip your house."

"I believe that's our cue to leave." Taylor and Drew hugged William and said their goodbyes before walking out into the cold night.

As she walked to the sidewalk, Taylor glanced up at the sky and spotted a twinkling star. She smiled believing it was a sign from her grandmother.

Drew opened the passenger side of his truck and helped Taylor inside. He then climbed into the driver's seat and started the ignition. The engine tumbled as the cab filled with heat and Christmas carols.

Taylor glanced at the brick ranch house. The lights in the foyer and living room were turned off. The house was in complete darkness until she spotted the light from the bedroom. She breathed a little easier knowing William was fine and about to snuggle in for a peaceful slumber.

"Ready honey?" Drew asked.

Taylor nodded. "Yeah."

"You worry about him don't you?" Drew pulled away from the curb.

"Since grandma died, I'm concerned about him being lonely."

"It's got to be difficult being alone in the house. But he's got us, and the rest of the family, so I think he'll be alright."

Taylor gave a faint smile. She noticed how excited he was at the party tonight. The joy on his face seeing his family gathered together and his great-grandchildren opening their gifts warmed his heart.

"Who knows, next year there might be an addition to the family," Drew replied as he slowed to a stop at an intersection.

Taylor's jaw dropped as she stared at her husband. They both wanted children, but they hadn't decided when to start trying. Hearing his suggestion caught her off guard, in a good way.

"I saw the gleam in your eye when you were playing with your nieces. You'd make an excellent mother, but it's up to you when the time's right." He pressed on the accelerator as he waited for a reply.

Taylor opened her mouth, but before she could a screeching sound filled the air as she felt a massive hit in her side. The truck spun around as glass flew everywhere and the next thing Taylor recalled was darkness.

Taylor's eyes fluttered as she was met with a bright light and a white tile ceiling. *Where am I? What happened?* She closed her eyes to shield them from the blinding light. Her mind raced with a million thoughts as the sound of IV drips and beeping machines filled the room.

*I'm in a hospital. But how did I get...*she remembered the car wreck. She and Drew were driving home when they were hit by another vehicle. "Drew."

Taylor's eyes popped open as panic coursed through her body wondering where her husband was. Her fingers clutched the bed as her toes wiggled. *I can move, that's a good sign.* Slowly Taylor raised up and to her surprise didn't feel any pain. She glanced down and saw she was still wearing jeans and her puppy Christmas sweater.

Guess, I didn't have any serious injuries. The impact probably knocked me out. Taylor's thoughts were interrupted when she heard a nurse walking by. "Excuse me," Taylor called out, but woman ignored her. *She's certainly rude.*

Doctors and nurses continued to stroll by paying no attention to Taylor. "Can someone help me? Anyone? I need to find my husband."

Frustrated with the lack of concern, Taylor decided to get out of bed. To her shock, there was no pain as she carefully walked into the hall. She looked down both ends as people passed by.

"Drew's got to be around here somewhere." Taylor walked to the left searching for the nurses station. Everyone continued walking without giving her any attention, almost as if she were invisible.

Nearing the end of the hall, she spotted Drew sitting in the waiting room. She blew a sigh of relief knowing her husband was fine. Confusion then replaced that joy when she saw her parents Susan and Chad.

"Don't tell me they came all the way down here in the middle of the night." She knew her parents were concerned after hearing about the accident. Knowing her mother, Susan had a fit and demanding updates. *Good luck with trying to get information from this staff.* "I'm fine everyone, no need to make a fuss."

Entering the area, Taylor noticed that neither Drew or her parents heard her. "I'm fine, we can go home now." Her words went unheard and nobody looked up at her. Drew and Susan wore worried expressions, while Chad put on his usual brave front, but his eyes showed sadness.

"It's my fault." Drew sniffled.

"Don't blame yourself." Susan gripped Drew's arm. "The officer said the other driver was texting."

"If we had left a little earlier…"

"Drew, calm down. It was an accident, it could've happened to either one of us."

Taylor shook her head at everyone's dramatics. "You don't have to worry, I'm fine." When she went to grab Drew's shoulder, Taylor was shocked to see her hand go through his body. "What the…?" She again tried to touch Drew, but was met with the same result. "Mom, dad, can you see me?" She waved her hands in front of her parents, but they ignored her just like Drew.

"What's going on? Am I dead?" Taylor pressed her hands against her forehead. *This can't be happening. This has got to be a dream. Yeah, a dream. I'll close my eyes and wake up in bed.* Taylor closed her eyes, hoping everything would be fine when she awoke. When she opened them, she was still at the hospital.

Drew jumped from his seat and walked through Taylor's spirit as the doctor came into the room. The force almost caused her to lose her balance, but she regained her composure.

"Doctor, how is my wife?" Drew wrung his hands.

"She sustained a cracked rib and a nasty cut on her forehead. She also has a few minor cuts, and luckily there is no internal bleeding."

Drew and Susan blew a sigh of relief at the news.

"She's in stable condition right now and we're monitoring her to make sure there are no further injuries."

"Can we see her?" Susan's voice took on a pleading tone.

"I'll have a nurse take you to her room. If you need anything, let me know."

"Thank you, doctor." Drew replied, then shot a look-up at the sky.

Taylor watched her family sig with relief, but she was befuddled. The doctor implied that she'd be fine, but why wasn't her spirit back in her body. *Am I dead? Or could I be in limbo? Maybe I'm technically not out of the woods yet.*

Her train of thought was interrupted when she saw the nurse taking her family to the room. Taylor trailed behind as the group entered the room she just came out of. Drew and her parents gathered around the bed, while Taylor halted at the doorway.

Her heart sank when she saw her body hooked up to the machines. A bandage covered the right side of Taylor's forehead, while small cuts and bruises decorated her arm.

"Oh, my God." She slowly walked toward the bed, moving to the side away from everyone else.

"It kills me to see her liked this." Drew gently touched his wife's hand.

"She's going to pull through. She a tough gal," Susan's voice cracked.

"She gets it from her mom." Chad hugged his wife, while trying to hold his emotions in. Like any parent he hated to see his child in pain, and could only imagine what Taylor was feeling.

"Don't cry," Taylor whispered, although she knew they wouldn't hear her. "I'm coming back to you." She carefully climbed back into her body, thinking this would wake her. She situated herself into a comfortable position and waited for the moment, her spirit would re-enter her body. Minutes passed and nothing happened, she figured the transition would happen quickly, yet she was impatiently waiting.

After a couple more minutes, Taylor's spirit arose out of bed. "This doesn't make any sense." Everything Taylor read about near death experiences, people claimed to see a white light guiding them to heaven. Yet, there was no white light for Taylor. "Maybe it's all a pile of rubbish."

The room filled with an alarm as Susan called for a doctor. Taylor watched in horror as the heart monitor flat lined and Drew's face filled with panic.

"No, Taylor, don't go," he shouted. "Fight baby, fight. Stay with us."

Doctors and nurses came rushing in, ordering the family to leave. Taylor watched as a doctor tried to resuscitate her.

"No." Tears brimmed her eyes refusing to believe she was dying. As the staff continued to work on her body, Taylor was blinded by a white light coming from her left side. She shielded her eyes from the light and noticed a woman's figure approaching her.

"Are you an angel?"

"Some people think I am," the woman replied.

Taylor's eyes widened at the sound of the voice, one she was familiar with, but hadn't heard in a long time. "Grandma?"

Slowly Taylor's hand moved from her eyes and she saw Grace standing before her. Grace wore the same pale pink suit she was buried in, and her white hair still in its natural curly state.

"Oh, my God, grandma." Taylor went to hug her grandmother and to her surprise, didn't pass through her. She basked in the warmth of Grace's embrace, happy to be with her grandma one last… "Wait, a minute. Have you come to take me…to Heaven?"

Taylor grasped Grace's hand as the looked at the doctor and nurses feverishly trying to save her. A tear fell down her cheek realizing this was probably the end. She knew when your time was up, it was time to go. While Heaven would be wonderful and she'd be reunited with Grace, she wasn't ready to leave.

There was still on Earth she wanted to do. She and Drew were talking about having children, but now they'd never see their dream of parenthood come true. Then there was her parents and grandpa, she couldn't fathom the thought of leaving her family behind.

Taylor broke down knowing that she was dead and never coming back. *Not like this. Why? Why now?* Feeling her grandma's gentle touch on her shoulder, Taylor's sobs dissipated.

"I guess it's time to go." Taylor held Grace's hand ready to be guided to the afterlife.

"Sorry, honey." Grace shook her head.

"I don't understand," Taylor rasped. "Didn't you come here to take me home?"

"Sweetie, I miss you like crazy." Grace caressed her granddaughter's cheek. "I'd love nothing more than to be with you. But it's not your time."

Relief swept over Taylor, but then confusion replaced it. "If it's not my time why am I stuck in limbo?"

"It happens with all spirits." Crave chuckled. "Many leave their bodies after an accident thinking they're dead, but not realizing it's not their time yet. That's why they need help from above to return."

"I tried it before, but it failed."

"This time it'll work. Trust me."

Taylor glanced at the bed, then back to her grandma. As much as she was ready to return, she also didn't want to leave Grace.

"Don't worry about me, dear." Grace squeezed her granddaughter's hand. "I'm fine. Heaven is a lovely place. I have my parents, my brother Albert, and all my cats and dogs to keep me company."

"I miss you, grandma. We all do."

"I know honey." Grace smiled. "But remember, although my body is gone, my spirit is still around. I'm still keeping a watchful eye on everyone, including you." She bopped Taylor's nose. "You've made me proud. It warms my heart seeing you look after grandpa and carrying on my family traditions."

Taylor beamed at her grandmother's kind words.

"You did an excellent job with the party." Grace nodded as Taylor went to speak. "Like I said, I'm still looking after you."

The tender moment was cut short by the doctor yelling "clear", then using the defibrillator.

"I think it's time to head back."

"Yes, my dear." Grace hugged Taylor, the two of them tightly embraced, not wanting the moment to end, but knew they had to say goodbye. "Remember to enjoy life. You've got a lot to be thankful for. Your family, Drew, and your daughter."

Taylor's eyes widened at the declaration. "Wait, I'm not preg…"

"You will be." Grace smirked. "Your little girl will come sooner than you think."

An emotional Taylor smiled at her grandmother's revelation, then touched her stomach. Before the crash, she was going to tell Drew she was ready for a family. Now they were going to have their chance to be parents. But first she needed to return.

"You better hurry." Grace's wrinkled hand waved toward the bed.

"Thank you, grandma." Taylor again hugged Grace, this time a brief embrace. "Goodbye."

"Goodbye, my dear. Remember, I'm always around."

Taylor watched as Grace disappeared back into the light. Then Taylor's spirit returned to the bedside. She gently climbed back into her body. This time when her spirit connected with her body, Taylor felt a warm, calming sensation envelop her.

The doctor yelled "clear" then pressed the defibrillator to Taylor's chest again. Her body jolted and her eyes shot open as the heart monitor beeped with activity.

Pain shot through Taylor's body as she tried to raise up. She was starting to feel the effects now. The pain was excruciating, but she took it as a reminder of how lucky she was to be alive.

Laying back down, she recalled the encounter with her grandmother. It was unbelievable. She read and heard about people's near death experiences. Never did she think she'd be one of those people.

A while ago she was hovering near life or death. But thanks to Grace's guidance, she had a second chance, one she wasn't going to squander. She vowed to cherish every moment in life, and she and Drew had many more memories to create.

Taylor's train of thought was disrupted by the door opening. She glanced at the entryway to see Drew entering. His oval face showed stress and his eyes were red.

"Hey baby." He gently kissed her left temple, he feared even the delicate touch would hurt her fragile frame. "You gave us quite the scare. Do you remember the accident?"

"I remember being hit and the truck spinning around. Then I blacked out." She reached out to touch his face. "How are you? Are you hurt?"

He shook his head. "I'm fine. Unfortunately, you were the only one hurt."

Taylor noticed his voice choking up. "Baby, don't cry."

"I can't help it." He grabbed a tissue from the table. "When you flatlined, I thought you were a goner. I couldn't fathom losing you. I prayed harder than I ever have." He glanced up at the ceiling. "I begged God not to take you. You had your whole life ahead of you and everyone needed you. I need you. You're my wife and best friend. I couldn't imagine life without you." His hand clutched the bed railing as he gazed at Taylor's face.

"Someone must've heard your prayers." Taylor wondered if she should tell anyone about her near death experience. While some people would believe her, skeptics would think it was a hallucination. It was a heartwarming experience, one she'd never forget, and one she decided to keep quiet, for now.

"You must've had an angel looking after you."

"I certainly did." She smiled. *An angel named Grace or as I like to call her grandma.*

"I'm thankful you're back." He carefully stroked her auburn hair. "The doctor wants to keep you here for a few days, then you can go home. But you've got to take it easy. I know how stubborn you are." Drew's voice took on an authoritative tone.

"Don't worry. With the way I feel, I won't be doing any strenuous work."

"Good to hear, your parents and I will make sure it that."

"Speaking of, where are they?"

Drew's face etched in confusion. "How did you know they were at the hospital?"

Taylor's mind quickly scanned for an excuse. "One of the nurses mentioned they were here."

"They'll be in soon." Drew looked toward the door, then back at Taylor. "They wanted to give me and you some time together. Do you want me to go get them?"

"Not yet." She reached out and took Drew's hand in hers. "Do you remember our conversation earlier, in the truck?"

Drew tried to recall their discussion. In all the chaos from the evening, his mind was drawing a blank.

"You asked if I was ready to start a family," Taylor replied.

"Honey, we can talk about that another time."

"I want to give you my answer." She ran her thumb across his knuckles and looked into his hazel eyes. "Yes, I'm ready to have a baby."

Drew's face lit up with the announcement. Overcome with excitement, he tenderly kissed his wife. "This has been an eventful night, while Christmas to be exact."

"This is one neither of us will ever forget." Taylor knew she wouldn't, and if her grandmother was right soon they'd have more special reasons to celebrate.

One year later...

Drew's truck pulled up to William's brightly lit house. Taylor's grandfather didn't do much decorating last year with the exception of a tree. But this year, he decorated the porch railings and posts with white lights and red bows. Taylor smiled at the sight, thankful her grandpa was back in a celebratory mood.

Drew opened Taylor's door, and helped her out. "Easy, honey."

"I'm fine, darling."

"You're still recovering." He opened the backseat and pulled out the baby carrier.

Taylor looked at her newborn daughter Grace dressed in red and white striped pajamas, with a little elf cap on her head. Taylor's grandmother was right when she said their daughter would arrive soon. Four months after the accident, Taylor and Drew found out they were expecting.

Drew immediately went into protective husband and dad mode. He made sure to attend every baby appointment, fixed Taylor her weird food cravings, and decorated the nursery. Although they weren't getting much sleep these days, Taylor wouldn't trade it for anything. The way Drew held their daughter and sung her lullabies warmed Taylor's heart. She couldn't ask for a better husband.

Baby Grace cooed at the lights as they walked up the pathway. Before they could knock, Susan flung open the door.

"There you are," she exclaimed. "Where's my granddaughter?"

Drew turned the carrier around so Susan could look at Grace.

"Oh, she's adorable in her Christmas outfit."

"We figured we'd get her started on the holiday traditions earlier." Taylor unhooked Grace from the carrier and gently picked up her daughter.

"It's hard to believe." Susan lightly pinched Grace's cheek. "Last year, I was at the hospital, worried if you'd..." she paused feeling like the waterworks were happening.

"Mom, it's okay." She wrapped her free arm around Susan. "I'm here now, and I'm fine. Well, except for a few sleepless nights," she giggled as Grace wiggled in her arms.

"You had an angel looking over you that night."

"I certainly did." Grace smiled then looked down at her daughter. Her grandmother was right in her prediction that she'd have a daughter. When Taylor learned they were having a girl, she knew what to name her.

"Is that Taylor and Drew?" William came out of the den. His cheerful demeanor, Santa hat, and green reindeer sweater filled the room with radiance.

"Hey, grandpa." Taylor kissed his cheek. "Good to see you're in a festive spirit."

"I have a lot to celebrate this year, including this little munchkin." William smiled at baby Grace who cooed with delight. "May I?" He held out his arms and Taylor carefully put Grace into his embrace.

Taylor watched William cradle Grace and play Goochie Goo.

"You're named after a wonderful woman." When he learned Taylor named the baby Grace, the honor touched his heart. If little Grace was anything like her great-grandmother, the world better watch out.

"I hope she grows up to be just like grandma."

William smiled and nodded at Taylor's words. Their sweet moment was cut short by Chad coming into the foyer.

"The kids are getting a little antsy, I think they're ready to open gifts." He glanced back at Mallory and Gina trying to keep them away from the tree.

"I think that's my cue." William held Grace as he entered the living room. "I think there's a special gift for a little lady."

Drew wrapped his arm around Taylor as they watched their daughter with her family. "I don't think we'll be seeing her for the rest of the night."

"Oh, we will. When she gets fussy or needs a diaper change, they'll be bringing her back." Taylor and Drew laughed.

Taylor watched as William sat in the recliner with baby Grace, and directed Chad on which presents to give out. Chad handed a small red bag with green tissue paper to William. The elderly man helped Grace unwrap it to reveal a white bear dressed in a pink sweater.

A feeling of bliss enveloped Taylor. She thought nothing could top last year's Christmas, but this year with baby Grace would be her most favorite.

"It's good to see you smiling." Drew nuzzled his wife's temple.

"I have a lot to be thankful for."

"So do I." Drew and Taylor often talked about the accident. During the first few weeks at home, he didn't want to leave her side. He was fretful that if he left, something bad would happen again. But once she was completely healed, he rested a little easier. However, his protective nature kicked into high drive now that they had a child.

Taylor gazed up into her husband's face, knowing he was thinking about her accident. "Let's not dwell on that, baby."

"I can't help it. It's been on my mind a lot. To think I almost lost you was frightening."

"It wasn't my time to go." She nestled her head into his chest. "My guardian angel had other plans for me." Taylor's focus moved to the angel tree topper. Her eyes squinted as she noticed a radiant glow emanating from it, and knew it was a sign. *I miss you too, grandma. Thanks for everything.*

Taylor smirked, happy to know her grandmother was around, watching them. But she hoped her grandma wouldn't see this next moment. Taylor coughed then nudged Drew's side.

"Something wrong, honey?" Drew's gaze followed Taylor's eyes gesturing toward the ceiling. He spotted the mistletoe and knew what was next.

Taylor wrapped her arms around Drew and kissed him as the warmth and magic of

Christmas surrounded them.

The End

Beth Freely, Carol Cassado, Ireland Lorelei, & Patricia

Mistletoe and Spurs

By Patricia Bates

Previously released as Christmas for the Cowgirl

Chapter One

Beyond the frosted pane of glass, a blanket of white lay over the land, ignored for the most part while Holly snapped the clasp on her travel case shut. A sweeping glance around the room revealed her neatly made king-sized bed, two oak dressers, and armoire. Each item had been lovingly cleaned in preparation for her week-long absence. She traced over the wedding ring quilt on the bed and tried to ignore the tremble in her fingers. Her stocking feet whispered over the thick Persian rug with each step she took toward the dresser. She lifted the small envelope that rested there.

"All set," she murmured to herself. She tucked her cellphone into her purse and started downstairs. The Christmas lights flickered and danced off the intricate rings on her fingers. Holly paused, her hand on the doorjamb, and looked around. A massive blue spruce sat decorated by the fireplace, a stack of wrapped parcels beneath it. Angels hung from ribbons to float above the room. It looked like the perfect Christmas scene, and she smiled slowly, a touch sadly.

Next Christmas would be different, maybe more luxurious, but she would have another miracle to celebrate. She inhaled and patted her still-flat abdomen. Oh yes, this year she'd gotten what she wanted for Christmas—but she had to find out if it was what he wanted.

Much the same as she'd done for the past six years, Holly meant to be away from home for the holidays. This would be her escape, her last chance to see if her relationship with Ty could survive. She loved him, that wasn't in doubt. No, it was something deeper, something darker. With a sigh she pushed the negative thoughts aside and turned off the lights. She tugged her rings from her fingers and dropped them into the ornate crystal bowl atop the foyer table before pulling on a pair of leather driving gloves and collecting her bags. With a final glance around, Holly started for the car.

The newer Chevrolet was something she hadn't originally intended to purchase, until she got the call from the doctor's office earlier in the week. She giggled and peeked into the mirror to wink saucily at her reflection. The everyday woman she usually saw had vanished. Instead, her artfully applied cosmetics gave her a sultry, seductive look. She reached up to pat at her plain brown hair, curled and piled up to enhance her cheekbones. She rubbed at her small nose to warm it from the cold as a cloud of mist escaped her painted lips with each breath.

"Well, girl, I say you are looking good. Let's see if anyone else notices." She blew herself a kiss and turned the engine over. She pulled the sturdy car out onto the highway and turned west.

* * * *

The drive into the city wasn't long by any means, but the empty highways allowed her time to let her mind wander. She tapped her nails to the beat of the George Strait tune drifting through the speakers. Road signs passed by in a blur of green and white, each a silent marker on the path to her future.

The white flakes that danced intermittently through the air only added to the holiday cheer. It would be an excellent skiing weekend, pure powder, but she had no plans to be outside during the holidays. The lines on the highway flashed past in the fading light, until the orange glow of the city lights came into view.

Hundreds of flickering lights skipped against a black backdrop like diamonds on velvet. Holly hit the turn signal and pulled off the nearly deserted highway. The car purred along the merge lane before gliding into the busy city traffic. She slowed down to a crawl and stared at the brightly lit storefronts and the strings of lights that hung from bare trees lining the streets.

The massive, decorated spruce that stood atop the hotel where she'd made reservations drew a giggle. It seemed fitting that the hotel would appear to be a gift. The holiday would be well worth the wait, she thought as she parked near the entrance.

"Good evening," the woman at the desk greeted her warmly. "Happy holidays."

"Merry Christmas," Holly replied, tucking her keys into her purse. "I'm Holly Walker. Is my room ready?"

"Yes, it is. Anthony will take your luggage up." The desk clerk waved a tall, sandy-haired young man over. "Will you be attending the auction tomorrow night?"

"Of course." Holly signed the slip with a flourish, a grin on her face. "I'm looking forward to it."

"Excellent. Enjoy your stay, Ms. Walker."

"Thank you." She followed the bellhop into the elevator. Holly stood silently, her gaze steady on the elevator doors. She could feel the young man's eyes on her, and she looked down at the pale flesh on her ring finger where her wedding band usually rested. She wondered if the elegant gold band would be back in place come Christmas morning.

With her luggage secured in her room, she pressed a bill into Anthony's hand and ushered him out the door. She tossed her coat across the back of a chair and turned to study her room.

A massive mahogany bed was made up in red and green linen. Six plump pillows lined the head of it and a bathrobe lay folded on the end. She ran a hand over the garment. The soft, warm fleece of the robe tickled her fingertips as her gaze swung to the desk in the room. A large, cellophane-wrapped basket sat atop it, and two crimson roses that had been tied with some holly hung from the handle.

She toed off her boots and padded on stocking feet to investigate the offering. The sweet scent filled her nostrils as she sniffed the flowers, her hand already reaching for the card. It was a simple card, elegant and very masculine in its stark whiteness and blueprint.

Merry Christmas, and welcome to the Mistletoe Charity Auction. I hope you'll find these small tokens useful. The masculine scrawl along the card curved upward to a seasonal graphic.

Holly tore into the goodies left by the hotel. A delicate flush climbed her cheeks as she pushed the cellophane away to reveal the contents of the basket. "No wonder it has dark wrapping." She whistled as she lifted out a bottle of massage oil. "Cherry flavored, hmm. Ooh, what's this?" She pulled out a slim package and turned it over. The simple silver box offered few clues to its contents. Her long nails scraped under the flap and pulled it upward. Inside lay a simple bottle. "Menthol lubricant, for that extra tingle." Holly laughed and set the bottle down next to the bed.

A quick glance at the clock revealed it was nearly seven. He must have arrived by now. Was he settled into his room, impatient for the culmination of their very own little ritual? She shifted, the bare skin of her thighs rubbing together to create a sweet, heated friction. Beneath the satin of her panties her body throbbed with a deep longing.

Desperate to hear his voice she grabbed her cellphone from the bedside table. Flipping it open, she stretched out on the bed. She slipped the fingers of her free hand between her legs to fan the flames as she punched in the familiar numbers. She listened to the musical tone of the ringer.

"Hello, you've reached Tyson. I can't come to the phone. Leave your name and number, and I'll be sure to call you back."

Holly trailed a finger down her throat as she listened to the rich twang in his baritone. At the beep she inhaled.

"Are you naked? Hard for me yet? I can't wait to taste you again," she purred. "I'm so hot and wet for you already. My fingers are wet with proof of my hunger. Mmm, it tastes so good." She moaned softly. She ran her tongue along her fingers before she hung up with a giggle and set her phone aside.

Holly arched her body as she moved on the bed. The friction of lace over the sensitive skin at her core sent a bolt of desire through her. She panted as she lifted her skirt. Her fingers circled, teased, pinched, and pulled at her swollen bud until she climaxed with a muted moan.

Still shaky she rose and stripped before she padded into the bathroom. The bathtub beckoned her, and she quickly filled it with water, adding in some salts and oils before sliding beneath the surface and lying back.

"Pick up candles before tomorrow night." She whispered the soft reminder as she closed her eyes and relaxed. A slow, steady smile crept across her face, and she snuggled deeper into the ornate tub.

* * * *

Tyson Walker pulled his Stetson down over his collar against the cold wind that blew off the frozen river. He shrugged deeper into his heavy winter jacket and jogged up the steps into the plain economy hotel where he was staying. Tired, cold, and hungry, he pulled the key from his pocket and strode past the desk clerk to unlock his door.

Small and simple, the room suited a single man completely. Two double beds took up most of the room. A plain dresser and table occupied the rest of the room, and a single-cup coffee station sat on a tray atop the table. "Decaffeinated coffee? They need to restock," he muttered, and reached for the small bag he'd carried. He pulled out a can of beer, and the pop as he opened it echoed in the room. Tossing aside his hat and coat, he stretched out, kicked his worn cowboy boots off, and wiggled his toes in satisfaction.

Tomorrow night would be the big deal. The main reason he'd come to town was for the charity auction, one that he felt honored to participate in. He reached for his phone and frowned at the blinking light.

"Who the hell would be callin' me? I told 'em not to bother me," he grumbled, flipping up the receiver. He quickly dialed up his voicemail and punched in the code. The sultry, seductive tone that filled his ears sent his blood racing to his groin. Fierce and powerful, the need to claim the voice's owner washed over him.

"Tomorrow, baby," he muttered as he slid his ring from his finger and tucked it into the band in his hat. He tipped the hat upside down and set it on the dresser next to his half-finished beer. The soft, honeyed tone that whispered in his ear sent a bolt of heat through his body. He could feel the blood rush from his head leaving him lightheaded. His flaccid penis twitched behind the tight denim, jumping as he closed his eyes imagining the curves that went with the voice.

Tyson reached for the snap of his jeans. The ache that filled him needed release, and there was only one way to do it. His eyes closed as he slid the zipper down over his rapidly growing hard-on. His erection hardened even further as he stroked it with the calloused palm of his hand. He pushed deeper into the pillow beneath his head, his free hand clutched the bedding. His fingers slowly eased around his hard-on, squeezing the base and loosening toward the head.

Behind his lids he saw her. Pale and sleeveless, her sundress caressed her legs as she twirled in the late day sun. The front dipped down between her breasts, the nipples hardened as she slipped the straps off her shoulders. Her hips swayed to the pounding of his heart. Waves of long brown hair cascaded down her back as she tipped her head back. Her hands cupped her full breasts. Long, pink nails pulled and pinched at the hardened nipples she held.

Soft grunts of pleasure filled the room as the rhythm of his hand around his member echoed that of his heart pounding. Soft, silky, the touch around his erection was familiar, yet different from his own. He could almost smell her perfume, taste the sweat that ran down her body in a silver trail. Tyson licked his lips as he imagined her fingers dipping beneath her waist to the trimmed curls at the apex of her thighs. Tightening and loosening, the actions sped up as his hips thrust into the motion of his hand. Using his own lubricant, the slide of his hand against the sensitive flesh of his penis pulled him closer and closer until he exploded, a groan slipping past his lips.

Tyson trembled as he shifted, his hips absently thrusting upward as he milked his length of any remaining fluids. Gasps for air slowed as his body calmed. The release had taken the edge off—for now, but it wouldn't last long. Sated, at least momentarily, he reached for the box of tissues that sat next to his bed and wiped himself clean. With an expert toss, the ball of used tissues sailed through the air into the wastepaper basket. He shimmied out of his jeans and kicked them aside before he stalked into the bathroom to have a quick shower.

Naked and still damp from the shower, he strode back to the bed and crawled in. He rolled over and slipped into a light sleep. A soft whisper echoed in the room as he called out to her.

Chapter Two

The worn denim hugged his thighs as Tyson hurried toward the main ballroom. Traffic had been a real bitch. Cars stuck in the freshly fallen snow had made for delays, and he was half an hour late. Waving a hand at one of the organizers, he pulled off his jacket and hung it up.

"Sorry, traffic problems," he explained as he cast a look around. The massive room had been sectioned off; screens stood around the room offering privacy to those who were changing. Chairs lined the wall, and tables were covered in a myriad of items. Down the center of the room, a row of tables with massive mirrors stretched out with several high-backed chairs spaced along its length.

"That's all right, honey." The woman smiled at him. "You have time to change, but you'll have to do it quickly. I'll have someone come oil you up." She trailed a hand over his arm, a look of appreciation and lust in her dark eyes.

Tyson smiled inwardly at the heated look in the blonde's eyes. With blue eyes and bleached blonde hair, she dressed to flaunt. Her red blouse gaped open to reveal the lace of her bra cups, mistletoe tucked into her cleavage. Her short skirt accented her long legs, and her red-heeled shoes only made them appear longer. She was an amazingly beautiful woman, but she wasn't the one he'd come for. "Sure. What am I wearin'?"

Her come-hither smile belied the innocence in her words. "Anything you can get into." She waved at the racks full of men's clothing and licked her lips as she sashayed past him.

Tyson snagged a pair of threadbare jeans and started for the change room. "I'll keep my boots on, ma'am."

Her soft giggle followed him. He ignored the other women and stepped into the small, screened-off change room. Stripped down to his briefs, he grabbed the jeans he was to wear and pulled them on. Tighter than he liked, they felt new, stiff, and ultimately uncomfortable. It was obvious that the denim was cut, not worn-through, and he wondered why he couldn't have just brought a pair of his old jeans instead. He eyed the rack of shirts for a moment before brushing past them. She liked him shirtless, liked to have at least some of him on public display for their game.

Under the firm direction of an older woman, he settled into a low-backed chair and watched the insanity around him. Men of all shapes and colors, dressed in various outfits, lounged around in jeans, fireman's pants, and a policeman's uniform. A tall, lean, dark-haired man dressed in a tuxedo sipped on a beer while he flirted shamelessly with one of the young women. Several others sat with fancy suits on, towels pinned around their necks while they had their hair styled.

"Seems a waste to be dressed like some slab of beef. All them fancy duds won't show the merchandise as well as bare flesh," he drawled as an older, red-haired man walked up, a bottle of oil in his hands. Ty waved at the activity around them while the man applied the warm, smooth liquid over his shoulders. "What's this oil for again?"

"Well, since you're not wearing a shirt, this will make those muscles of yours stand out under the lights. A little something to attract more bids, which will mean more money for the charity."

Tyson turned to look at the man rubbing the oil over his body, his eyes narrowing with an unspoken challenge. "Be careful where you put those hands. That's a fresh wound." He stared at the jagged, angry line that marred his tanned skin—an unnecessary reminder of the dangers of being a bull rider.

"Don't worry. I do this for a living." He grinned. "I'm Rudy, a massage therapist. And even a blind man could see that scar is new."

"Massage therapist?" Tyson nodded thoughtfully. He glanced at the man when he chuckled and raised an eyebrow. "If you're implyin' I meant anything…"

"Not implying anything. I work with accident victims, sports injuries, that sort of thing." Rudy grinned. "I see you've got quite the collection of scars. You an athlete or something?"

"Yeah, or something." Tyson frowned at the reminder of what he'd been, what he was still considered to be. He just didn't know if he could live up to the hype that going to the Rodeo

Nationals brought with it. "So what are you doing down here?"

"I'm donating a few hours of my time for a worthwhile cause. This year the proceeds are going to the local hospital. My daughter spent three months there this past year undergoing surgery. This is my way of giving back, especially since my wife won't let me volunteer to be a date."

"Wise woman." Tyson shifted in the chair.

"Indeed. So what brings you here?"

"Figured I'd help out a worthy cause," Tyson replied with a grin. "Actually, once a year I try to do something big for someone. This year, well, why not get auctioned off for a Neonatal Intensive Care Unit?"

"Thanks, man. Your help is appreciated, even if it never feels like we say it enough. They'll want you over in hair." Rudy patted him on the shoulder. "Now that you're all oiled up and glistening."

Tyson laughed softly and rose. He walked across the floor, dodging people, costumes, and the occasional woman. He eyed a pretty redhead who smiled at him and held up a bottle of gel.

"This won't hurt a bit, and it'll make you look even sexier," she promised. "I'm Phyllis, by the way. I saw you talking to my husband."

"Ahh, you're Mrs. Rudy." Tyson shot her a quick grin.

"One and the same." She rubbed the gel between her hands and set to work making his wavy hair stand up in odd directions. "I see Helen didn't give you the rest of your costume." Phyllis nodded at the workstation before her. "Take one of the bowties, you'll be wearing it with your, um, costume."

"Sorry, ma'am, but I'm not the kinda guy you get into a tie. Jeans and a work shirt are about it for me," he explained. "I ride bulls and broncs for a living."

"Bulls and broncs? What do you mean?"

"I'm a rough stock rider for the rodeo circuit," Tyson explained with a grin. "I got banged up pretty badly and missed out on Finals this year."

"Well, it's nice to have you here." Phyllis paused at the static voice coming over the speakers. "Looks like they're getting ready to start this thing, you'd better get a move on, good lookin'. Good luck."

"Thanks."

Tyson headed for the staging area. The women whispered around the assembled bachelors, giggles and whistles filling the air. He paused at one subtle whisper and hid a smirk. His attention drifted downward to his left hand. Regardless of his attire, he couldn't help but feel naked without that simple band of gold. He flexed his fingers slightly before moving forward to stand between the 'fireman' and the 'tuxedo'.

* * * *

Holly stepped before the full-length mirror in the corner of her suite. She rolled her shoulders and straightened. Her hair, piled atop her head and cascading in curls down past her shoulders, was sexy and alluring. The gold and brown eye shadow gave her a sultry, exotic look. Her ruby lips tilted upward in a smile as she assessed the daring gown she'd made especially for the evening.

Made from gold satin, it clung to every curve, sliding across bare flesh like a lover's caress. The shimmering material dipped down to her navel, revealing more than an ample amount of her full breasts. There was no back to speak of, just a few thin, sequined straps that crisscrossed. She turned, a slow seductive smile across her face. The high slit bared her thigh almost to her hip.

"Good thing I don't have any underwear on," she muttered as she adjusted the strap on her stocking. Satisfied with her appearance, Holly picked up her plain wrap and pulled it tight. Her small clutch glittered in the light before she turned the lamps off and stepped into the hallway.

Her eye caught the lusty stares of two young men standing in the hallway. She felt the heat of their gazes as they watched her walk to the elevator. She ignored their indistinct and hurried whispers as she stepped past the automatic doors. Soft classical refrains filled the steel box as it descended to the main floor. She stepped out and strolled along the walkway, her eyes scanning the room quickly.

A large tree sat in the corner, white lights blinking merrily. Beneath it sat a pile of brightly colored boxes. Hung throughout the room were strands of garland wrapped in small white lights. Classical Christmas music filled the room with soft, soothing tones. Brilliant red curtains hung down, obscuring an area from view. Like an arm reaching out, a massive, black stage glistened in the lights.

"Good evening. Can I help you?"

Holly turned to the young woman standing beside her in a red velvet dress. A sprig of holly decorated the left side of her dress, held in place by a tiny Santa brooch. "I'm here for the auction."

"Oh, of course." A bright smile crossed the woman's face. "My name's Tanya, I'm one of the coordinators. If you'd like to register, it's this way. We do ask that everyone demonstrates the ability to meet their bids."

"Thank you, Tanya, but I've already registered. My name's Holly Walker, I believe you've already received my information."

Tanya shifted, her eyes widening as she flipped through the pages on her clipboard. "Oh, Ms. Walker, I uh didn't recognize you. Forgive me, I'm not overly familiar with all the registration cards. I've been handling the props and such. If you registered and submitted the information requested then we should have you on file. I can check that for you. Do you have your invitation?"

"I do." Holly pulled the card from her handbag and handed it over.

Together they walked across the room to where a long table sat. Holly surveyed the room, her attention on the other women milling about, while Tanya looked up the information.

"Here we go, Ms. Walker." Tanya handed her a card with a number on it. "I hope you'll have fun."

"I'm sure I will. Good luck with the event." Holly walked across the room and settled at a table close to the stage. She set her bag on the table and shrugged out of her wrap. A warm hand curved over her shoulder. Startled, she glanced up into the smiling gaze of a young woman dressed in a tuxedo.

"Wine?"

"No, thank you, I don't drink," Holly declined gracefully. "Would you please bring me a tonic water or something non-alcoholic?" She crossed her legs carefully as several other women joined her at the table. Holly greeted them all politely, distantly, as the lights dimmed and static suddenly filled the room.

A tall, dark-haired man with graying temples stepped out onto the stage and cleared his throat. "Good evening, ladies. I hope you're all here with open hearts and wallets." Laughter swelled around the room, followed by a round of applause. "We're here to show some holiday spirit and help a very worthwhile cause. It is our intention to raise two hundred thousand dollars in the next two years. I have to say that the balance has gone up from the last fundraiser. We now have sixty-two thousand, nine hundred and four dollars and sixteen cents. It's a good start. Remember, each of our gentlemen have a preplanned date for the lucky bidder." His gaze swept around the room.

Holly shifted as the man straightened slightly.

"Have fun, be safe, and keep those check books open. I'll turn the event over to Tanya, our evening's emcee and one of the women responsible for putting this together."

"Thank you, Scott. Welcome, ladies, to tonight's festivities. Our first victim for the evening will be Jason Lewis," she said as the curtains parted and a tall, muscular man dressed as a fireman stepped out. "He's a volunteer fireman here in town. Loves cats, kids, and ice cream. Come on, ladies, let's start the bidding at two hundred!"

Holly sipped her water calmly, trying to ignore the catcalls and whistles from the women around her. She carefully eyed each man as he stepped past the curtain. She was growing impatient and wished things would speed up. Her eyes darted down to check the time, curious to know how long she'd been watching grown women act like kids at an ice cream truck. A glance at her watch revealed the auction was nearly wrapped up. She smiled into her glass—very soon the wait would be over.

"And now for those ladies who haven't got a date. We have a treat. All the way from Hornbow ranch, we have a real live cowboy." Tanya waved a hand at the curtain as it parted to reveal the shadowed figure of a man.

Holly swallowed, her gaze soaking in the sight before her. A dark felt Stetson sat at a rakish angle on his head. His broad shoulders flowed down into a chiseled torso; a matting of darker hair followed a familiar line down his body, disappearing into the low riding Levis he wore. The long, tight jeans were threadbare in places, leaving little to the imagination. Her mouth went dry as she noticed the way he was 'dressed'. The faded lines of the denim flowed down along the ridge they hid, to the edge of the frayed spot near his upper thigh. With each step he took, she could see the muscles flex and ripple beneath the material. A large championship buckle sat in the middle of his lower abdomen, the edges of his flanks visible as he pulled the pants down with his thumbs in the belt loops.

A pair of shiny spurs decorated the worn black boots on his feet. Each step sent a faint but distinctly metallic jingle through the air. The tall man stopped at the end of the runway. He lifted the toe of one boot and rocked it back and forth in a slow, beckoning motion.

"Starting bids?" Tanya paused to cast an appraising stare at the man standing beside her. "How about two hundred? That's a real championship buckle, ladies. He was the bronc riding champion of 2007, as well as came in the top three in bull riding. Gals, this is a man who knows how to stay in the saddle."

"Two hundred!" a voice rose from the back of the room.

"I have two hundred," Tanya called. "Two twenty?"

"Three hundred," another voice chimed in.

Holly smirked into her glass as she watched the other women in the room wave their cards about. As the bids rose higher, she sneaked a glance at the man standing silently on the runway. His expression hadn't altered, his stare scorched through her dress, kindling the desire that was never far away.

"One thousand dollars," someone called.

He didn't move a muscle, just stood there silently, his hat pulled low. The faded denim of his jeans hugged the strong, hard length of his legs as he altered his stance to tempt her just a bit more.

Holly shifted, uncrossed and re-crossed her legs. Noting the way his pale eyes followed the gesture, she adjusted her dress a bit to reveal more leg. With each movement he swallowed, his body tensed, and he shifted slightly in an attempt to hide his reaction.

"Twenty-five hundred dollars." Holly waved her sign when he stuck his hands deep into his pockets. The motion pulled his jeans tighter, and an ache settled deep within her. She wondered if anyone would notice a damp spot on her dress. Her breasts tightened, her nipples hardening to poke at the slinky fabric of her gown. Unashamed of her arousal, she stared at him; her gaze followed his tongue as he licked at his lips.

A shocked hush fell over the crowd as everyone turned to stare at her. Slowly, murmurs began to swarm around the room. Speculation flew as the other women assessed her. She merely sipped at her drink, her gaze steady as she stared at the cowboy on display.

"Any other bids?" Tanya asked weakly. Silence descended as she searched for any other bidders. Finally, after a few moments of stunned stillness, she brought the gavel down. "Twenty-five hundred dollars it is. Sold to the lady in gold."

Holly smirked to herself and stood. She collected her wrap, clutch, and auction card. With a final parting glance at her 'date', she slipped through the throng of women toward the exit. A young man with a clipboard appeared beside her, a smile on his face.

"Could you fill this out?" he asked softly.

Holly took it, filled everything out, and reached into her reticule. "Cash okay?"

"Cash, ma'am?" he croaked as she pulled a wad of bills from her purse.

He watched, bug-eyed, as she counted out twenty-five one hundred dollar bills and laid them atop the clipboard. His eyes followed her movements as she pulled out a red fifty and tucked it into his pocket. "Would you be so kind as to ensure that I get a receipt, please?"

"Yes, Ms. Walker, I'll leave one for you at the front desk. Are you checking out tonight?"

"No, I've booked my room for a few days," Holly explained, and sauntered off. Sidestepping the hovering waiter by the door, Holly dodged the milling crowd, pausing at the edge of the stage to wink at her 'date' before putting an extra swing in her step and leaving the ballroom.

The elevator pinged its annoying sound as the doors swung open, and she stepped inside, aware of the silent man standing inches from her bare back. Careful not to catch her stiletto heels on the edge of the track, she turned to catch her date's lust-filled gaze. His shadow loomed in behind her, and she reached for the panel. Her long-nailed finger pressed her floor number and she peeked upward, her body abuzz with sensations, desires, and she wondered if this time would be any better than the others.

Silence filled the elevator as it climbed to her floor. The doors swooshed open, and Holly headed for her room. She could feel the heated breath that whispered along her bare back as a shadow strode a step behind. Key in hand, Holly stared at her door for a moment before she unlocked it. With the door held open, she waited for her guest to step inside before closing it with a soft click. The green *Do Not Disturb* sign swung from the door handle.

Chapter Three

Tyson grinned as he watched his 'date' reach for the bottle of chilled wine. A fine tremble raced over her flesh, and her hands shook as she poured two glasses and held one out to him.

Her painted lips puckered around the edge of the glass, the lipstick glistened teasingly at him. He hid the slow slide of his smile when he took a sip and set his glass down.

Confidently, he reached up and pulled his hat off. The dark Stetson sailed across the room to land with a thud in a chair, forgotten for the moment.

"Nice room," he drawled, his gaze settling on the king-sized bed. His body stirred, hardened while he stared at the plush mattress and bedding. Desire, thick and hot, raced through his blood when she shrugged, the movement causing the strap of her dress to slip a bit.

The pale curve of her breast peeked at him, and the friction of tight denim on his hardened manhood created an ache. Tyson watched her move, the silk of her gown rising and falling with each breath. Each inhalation sent the material sliding a bit more, until it seemed to hang on the hardened tips of her full breasts.

His gaze landed on the basket that sat by the bed and he moved to investigate. His work-roughened hands picked their way through various oils, boxes, and several strings of condoms. "Interesting gift basket."

"I thought so," she replied softly. "A few really interesting items in there. Have you tried the mint?"

Tyson picked up the small bottle with several tiny green leaves wrapped around it and read the label before setting it next to the bed. "Not yet."

"So, cowboy, what did you have in mind for this date?" The conversational tone was at odds with the lust in her gaze and her short, shallow breaths. Her red-tipped nails traced invisible lines along her cleavage, dipping down under the fabric before trailing back up.

"I thought we could stay in." He reached out with a finger and eased the strap of her dress down a little further on her shoulder, leaving the silk hanging off a turgid nipple. "After all, I'm starving."

Throaty and flirtatious, her chuckle warmed him and he shifted, his hand going to adjust his erection. Tyson reached for her glass and sat it on the table next to his. He stepped closer to her, his gaze darting over the uncovered flesh. One hand moved up to trail across her graceful neck and tangle in the mass of curls behind her head. He felt the shudder that raced through her body. Her flesh puckered into gooseflesh when he blew across it.

Tyson met her eyes, watched the pupils dilate even further and the lust stand out. Her lashes lowered to half-mast. A flush climbed her cheeks. A tiny gasp escaped her as he leaned forward, the stubble of on his chin scraping along the column of her throat.

Spicy and erotic, the aroma of her perfume rose in a cloud around him. He breathed it deep into his lungs and wallowed in the familiarity. He trailed his lips across her jaw to her ear. The lobe slipped into his mouth easily. He nibbled and suckled it until she clutched at his biceps. His tongue tangled with the diamond stud in her ear, moving it within the small hole delicately. With his teeth nipping at the flesh, he chuckled at her moan. A tortured groan slipped past her lips as he pressed a hot, moist kiss below her ear. He trailed down the smooth skin, his nose buried in her hair. Suddenly, he grabbed at the tender flesh and bit down gently.

A small cry of pleasure echoed in his ear as her nails dug deep into the muscles of his arms. Her hair cascaded over his arm as his fingers crawled into the knot of hair to knock the pins loose. He pulled gently, tilting her head to expose more of her pale neck. He nibbled down the column to lick at her pulse.

Tyson shifted, his groin rubbing against her leg as she slid a hand down his torso to cup his length beneath the denim. He groaned in pleasure as she squeezed him, her hand moving along the hardened length to create a sweet, painful friction of denim and flesh. His fingers tangled in the fabric of her dress and pulled it down, catching her arms to leave them trapped around her waist. Hot and moist, his lips moved down her body. He drew the tip of her breast into his mouth, laving the plump, heaving flesh with his tongue. He bit down, and his blood throbbed with desire at her muted groan. He dragged his teeth across her flesh before letting the mass slip from his lips and then diving back in, worshipping her breasts. His teeth caught around the turgid tip and tightened, moving from side to side. Her responses were so different from the usual moans and cries; he briefly wondered why she was so sensitive before lust steamrolled curiosity.

Her grip tightened around him, painful, yet so pleasurable. His free hand crept up her ribs to cup her other breast. He manipulated the orb, tweaking and twisting the nipple with careless abandon. Her cries of pleasure and the flexing of her fingers drove him on. Her hand moved up to cup his head, the nails scratching along his scalp. Her fingers tangled and tugged at his hair. Tyson pressed open-mouthed kisses along her abdomen, down to the tangle of fabric.

With his gaze locked on hers, Tyson slid down her body. Tortured groans escaped them both as he knelt before her. He pushed the lightweight, slinky material to one side and slipped a hand over her silk stockings to trace her hip. He chuckled when he realized the only attire she wore underneath her dress was her garters and stockings. His tongue slipped out to lick along her folds, tasting her. He moaned his appreciation of the sweet, heavenly moisture that glistened between her legs.

A sudden shudder from her and he tasted more of her. She clutched at his hair, her fingers tangled within it as she arched into his tongue. "Oh God! Please…" she cried out. "I'm so close, don't…don't stop."

Tyson pressed against her aroused bud. The friction and vibrations were enough to send her careening over the edge with a jolt. Her cry filled his ears with satisfaction. A final swipe of his tongue and then he stood. Bending his knees, he lifted her off her feet. Automatically her legs wrapped around his waist, her arms around his neck as she stared at him.

He leaned forward and pressed a desperate, demanding kiss to her lips. He forced his tongue between her lips, letting her taste herself as he lowered her to the bed. Her heels dug into his back as he slid her across the satin cover before straddling her hips, his erection straining against the zipper of his jeans.

Rocked back on his heels, he stared at the dazed, heated look in her eyes. He couldn't help the smug feeling that crept over him. He reached for the buckle on his belt and undid it slowly. Inch by inch, he pulled the thick strap of leather free of the loops and tossed it aside. She stared at him as he slipped the button free and pushed the heavy denim down past his hips.

He groaned in pleasure at the release from the confining material and kicked the denim off his legs. His erection jumped at the heated look in her eyes. Hungrily, Tyson watched her struggle with her emotions, the heave of her breasts, as she trailed a hand over her body.

"That's it, touch yourself. I want to see you lose control, baby. Bring yourself to the edge," he whispered gutturally as he stroked himself. He stared as her fingers drew lazy patterns over her flesh, her long red nails leaving faint white lines. She groaned as she slid them through the curls at the apex of her thighs.

Tyson ran his hand up her legs, his fingers pausing as they encountered the small, intricately drawn Celtic tattoo. Tiny shocks raced through her flesh, making it dance beneath his caress. Muscles jumped and twitched as he soothed them with light touches. He grinned to himself as he stared at the bold swirling lines decorating her flesh. He hadn't seen it until now, and it had been well worth the wait.

Her soft cry was full of desire and need when she arched into her own touch.

"Do you want me?" Tyson choked out. "Do you need me?"

"God, yes. Please, Ty." She flushed at the slip but lurched into his touch nonetheless. It was a mark of pride for him to know he made her lose so much control that she ignored one of the more g-rated rules to their play—no using their full names, stay in character.

Tyson smiled and pressed a kiss to her hip before he leaned over her and grabbed the string of condoms from the bedside table. Their eyes locked as he slowly rolled it on. Desire and lust tangled with excitement. She whimpered as he slid into her. Suddenly he pulled out, his fingers sliding along her swollen folds. Held prisoner by his gaze, she gasped and writhed on the bed as he slid a finger into her. He crooked it, pressing upward as he moved it slowly over her depths. Her muted cries and whimpers drove him relentlessly.

She whined a protest as he slid his fingers from the warm wetness of her body. Their eyes locked as he trailed them up over her flushed skin, leaving an invisible line he followed with his lips. Her full, pouty lips parted as he shifted his body, moving upward to hover over her. Tyson stared at the lust clouded expression in her eyes and reached for his turgid length. Slowly, he moved into place and guided his hardness into her hot sheath.

They both shuddered as his penis slid inch by inch into her moist depths. He grunted as she arched up into his thrust. Buried deep within her, Tyson groaned as she wrapped her legs around his hips and rolled, locking his hands behind her ass as she sat up, forcing him deeper. The soft satin of the covers tangling beneath him slid across his flesh as she rocked back and forth on his erection.

Her fingers tangled in the bedding as she rode him. The sensations of silk on his bare skin had his member hardening even more. He struggled to ignore the throbbing of his erection, choosing instead to focus on her. The tiny ripples of her internal muscles along his cock revealed how close she was to the edge. Roughly, he pulled out of her and rolled, pinning her beneath him. Each gasp, each moan was one step closer to the edge of oblivion. Her back arched, her hands clutched at the bedspread, and her heels dug into his buttocks. Perspiration clung to her skin, and a delicate flush flooded her features and breasts. The full globes heaved with her breaths. He laved each nipple, biting and sucking until he felt her explode.

His control shattered with each wave of her release over his hard cock, Tyson lurched forward once. Twice. He groaned as he buried his face in her shoulder. Minuscule aftershocks raced through them both as they struggled to get their breathing under control.

Moaning softly in protest as his flaccid penis slipped from her body, Tyson shifted. He rolled away from her and disappeared into the bathroom. After disposing of the used condom, he ran warm water in the sink and dipped the face cloth into it. It was a familiar ritual, one that he'd established early in their sexual relationship. He padded back into the bedroom and moved to her side. Using the warm cloth, he cleaned her carefully, his touch light and caring before he tossed the wet cloth into the bathroom. He crawled onto the bed and pulled her into his arms.

"Hmm, the heat feels so good," she whispered sleepily, her fingers laced with his. "Thank you."

Tyson smiled into her hair and reached for the spare cover that lay tangled at the foot of the bed. He pulled it over them and slid into a deep, sated sleep.

* * * *

Holly shifted against the warmth behind her. She blinked and stretched. Her body felt heavy, languid. As always, great sex had relaxed every muscle in her body. She turned to the figure behind her and smiled. A light snore broke the silence as his chest rose and fell with each deep breath. The signs of worry were gone from his features.

She slipped from his grip and padded into the bathroom. Turning on the heat-lamp, she looked in the mirror. Her hair and makeup were a little worse for the wear. Sweat had made her mascara run, and her hair was a tangle of knots and pins. Her fingers made short work of the pins, and she turned to run a hot shower. The sound of her stomach rumbling reminded her she hadn't eaten in hours. While the water heated she reached for the bathroom phone.

"Front desk."

"Is the kitchen still open?" she asked quietly.

"Yes, it is. What can I get for you?"

"Could you please send up two BLT sandwiches on white, one with fries, the other with salad. And a pot of coffee."

"Certainly, ma'am. Will there be anything else?"

"Yes, I'd like an extra set of bath sheets." She picked up a small bottle on the counter and read it. She tucked the phone into her shoulder and sniffed at the lotion before putting it aside. "Was there a set of bags delivered earlier?"

"For you, ma'am?"

"The initials on them would be TW."

"Yes, ma'am, they've arrived. We're waiting for them to be picked up."

Holly smiled. "Thank you. Please have them delivered to my room. And there should have been a dry cleaning bag brought by. A Santa suit?"

"I'll send them both up, Ms. Walker."

"Excellent." Holly hung up the phone and pushed the curtain aside. She stepped into the warm spray and sighed. The heat of the water washed away the makeup, the hairspray, everything that she'd plastered on to be someone other than herself. Holly rolled her neck under the shower, her hand already scrubbing at the streaks of black mascara that trailed along her body. The familiar smell of rosemary filled the room as she used the hotel's shower gel to cleanse away the painted lady.

After washing her hair, she turned off the water and stepped out of the shower stall to smile at the man who held a bath sheet open for her. "I didn't mean to wake you."

"You didn't," he replied, and pulled her closer to him.

She responded to his gentle kiss before she tucked her head under his chin. "I've ordered something for us to eat." She pressed heated kisses along the tanned flesh before her.

"Good, you're gonna need the energy," he teased, and swatted her on the rump as she scurried out of the bathroom. "Did you get coffee?"

"It's on its way, along with your luggage," Holly called back, and opened her suitcase. She pulled out the red silk nightie she'd made and slipped it on. The comforting sounds of the shower filled the room as she moved the wine off the table and cleared the top in preparation for the room service delivery.

When it arrived, she paid the tab, tossed in a tip, and set it down as the bathroom door opened and her lover stepped out. He leaned against the doorjamb and watched her. "Does your husband know where you are?"

Holly rolled her eyes thoughtfully. "Does your wife?"

Tyson chuckled and moved to hold her close. "You know what time it is?" he whispered, his attention on the digital clock.

Holly turned in his embrace and shrugged. "So? I'm usually just going to bed at this time. I have a good excuse for being up this late."

He eyed the clock, skeptical before he offered a quick grin. "Food, woman. You need the calories. The night's still young—and I'm starving."

Holly laughed and sat down on the edge of the bed. She took the plate from his hands and set it in her lap. "So, cowboy, tell me about yourself."

"I ride rough stock. Broncs, bulls in the CPRA." He paused and looked at her. "You know what that is?"

Holly shrugged, fully at ease with this particular game in their annual ritual. "Figure it's something to do with rodeo. Go on."

Tyson spoke clearly, detailing his exploits of the past year until the accident. "That bull's a prize-winner. Never been ridden, and I thought I could beat him. I wanted to finish the year in grand style, to be top ranked for the Finals, but it didn't work out that way."

"So, what are you going to do if you can't go back?" Holly tossed her napkin onto the empty plate and set it aside. His answer was important, and she waited impatiently to hear it. Despite their role-playing, this conversation had far-reaching consequences that could alter her future drastically. She shifted to hide the tremble in her body, the fear that raced along her nerves.

"I don't know. I've never done anything but rodeo, so not being able to do it is kinda hard."

Holly nodded. "What about ranching? Why can't you do that?"

Tyson stared at her, a multitude of emotions on his face. "It's not the same. We run a small ranch when I'm not on the circuit."

"What does your wife say about this? Doesn't she resent having you only a few nights a year? I mean, you're my lover and I could do with more than a few weekends. Is it enough to keep your relationship together?" She pointed at the pale band of skin around his ring finger.

"She wants me to stay home, to ranch. Sure, I'd like to be able to be home every night, but the road has some real perks to it. There's a wildness, an untamed quality to it. When we're together it's great. The sex is great, the laughter, the conversations, but..." Tyson shrugged uncomfortably. "I just don't think I can ever stay put. Moving from place to place is something I've always done. I can't stop being me."

Holly nodded carefully; her eyes dropped to her lap. It was a familiar refrain, one she'd heard before, and she felt her heart break a little. Sometimes it was an uphill battle to be the strong one, to be the one that waited. Now was one of those times. "So, you'll continue chasing the circuit then?"

"I'm not sure. I'm headed home in a few days, and after that I'll see."

Holly smiled and shrugged. These few days weren't about choices that affected them in real life. This was her time to be a woman. Her chance to be sexual, to explore the dangerous side of her desires without worry or concern for the consequences. She pushed her disappointment aside and smirked at him. The bed shifted beneath her as she got on her knees and reached for the plate in his hands. "Well, let's see if we can fit a few more hours of excitement in, shall we?" she whispered, and leaned forward to kiss him.

Chapter Four

    Holly giggled to herself as she adjusted her Santa's hat. Behind her, in various places, candles flickered softly. The pale light lit the room in dancing waves of gold and orange. She picked up the red bustier and slipped it on. Expertly, she fluffed the white faux fur that lined the top of it. Her completed attire included a pair of scandalous red panties. The thin strips of fabric revealed more flesh than they covered.

    She stared down at her skimpy clothes, turning slightly to ring the tiny bells on the sides. Situated right above her folds was a graphic of mistletoe. She wondered if he would catch that. Satisfied that she looked her best, she ran her fingers through her hair and crawled onto the bed. Beside her, in a cup of hot water, a bottle of oil sat warming. Soft music filled the room with a romantic touch.

The sound of the key card unlocking the door drew a smile as she rubbed her foot against her leg and lounged back. She smothered a giggle at the shocked look on Tyson's face. It faded, replaced by lust, so quickly she wasn't even sure it had been there.

He peeled off his winter wear and let it fall as he strode toward the bed. Worn leather came off as easily as snake's skin with each step. Her gaze never left him, and as she watched, his eyes darkened and his features became hard and set with desire.

Arousal, hot and wet, settled low within her body. She shifted, the thong rubbing along her folds to stir the need. Her rapt gaze was steadfast as she watched his fingers slide the buttons free from the holes to expose the tanned flesh of his torso.

She made a strangled sound of protest when he reached for his belt. Her fingers shook as she eased his away. Gazes locked, she slowly worked the belt buckle loose and slid the leather from around his waist. A grin crossed her face as she dropped it, the thud satisfying.

"What's on your mind, you witch?" Tyson whispered.

"Shh, it's my turn." She pressed soft kisses to his chest, her nails raking through the hair at his groin. The hiss of his breath as she slid his jeans off resonated within her body, heat pooling between her legs.

She nibbled at his chest, laving his nipple with soft licks. She wallowed in his muted groans of pleasure. His hands tangled in her hair, a fierce glint in his eyes. She held steady as she moved lower, her nails trailing across his flesh.

She licked along the faint jagged scar that ran from his ribs to his flank. His muscles followed the smooth line of a scar along his hip, and she nipped at it. Her strained breathing filled the room as she pushed the remainder of his attire from his body.

A low desperate growl rumbled through his chest as she traced over his hard length. Her nails scored along the delicate tissue between his legs, and his eyes flashed dangerously. Need and craving shone from his eyes as they followed her every movement.

Slowly, tortuously, Holly eased him deep into her mouth. Her tongue danced over the sensitive flesh, following the natural lines along his erection. Again and again, she drew him in and out, her eyes fastened on his gaze.

Shocked laughter filled the room when he roughly pushed her backward. The thrill of his dominant act added to her already heady arousal. She leaned back on her elbows, her legs crossed teasingly. She shivered at the heat and feral glint in his gaze. A squeak of alarm slipped past her lips when he grabbed an ankle and jerked her forward.

"You, lady, are a tease," he ground out. Hands that showed none of the tenderness of the night before grabbed her panties and tore them from her body. "Do you know what happens to a tease?"

Holly tipped her head back and laughed. She raised one foot and pushed against him. "No, tell me," she whispered and climbed to her knees. A shiver of anticipation and desire skittered up her spine at the play of emotions on his face.

His harsh kiss swallowed her gasp when he picked her up and pushed her against the wall. His hot breath feathered over her skin as he leaned forward to whisper in her ear. With each salacious, crude word she shuddered, her body hung on the precipice of release. His fingers darted along her body, ripping the laces loose on her underwear and shoving them aside.

She reached for him and curled her palms around his shoulders. Her fingers scratched at his back as he slid into her. The weight of his body pressed the air from her lungs, and she gasped and moaned. Suddenly, he grabbed her hands. His fingers laced with hers to pin them to the wall behind her head. Determined to claim her own satisfaction, Holly ground herself against the hardness buried inside her core.

Each moist nudge drew strangled moans from them. A roll of her hips, a thrust of his hips and he slid into her wet heat. She tightened her legs around him, eased herself upward before she sank down upon him. Inch by inch she eased down until his erection was buried inside her.

"Still a tease?" Her teeth sank into his bottom lip and she bit down. His low growl grew as she pulled back and her teeth slipped off. She caught his wince and smirked as she realized it had stung. He thrust hard into her. She shuddered and moaned her approval. "Harder, Tyson, harder."

Tyson's groan echoed in her ears as his movements slowed. He shifted, braced himself, and withdrew to pound into her. Faster, faster, harder and harder, he drove her into the wall.

Tighter. Tighter. *Tighter.* Like a spring wound too tightly, tension built within Holly's body. Lost in the wash of sensations, she felt the friction of the curls at their joining. The coldness of the wall at her back. The sting of his teeth in her neck. His hot breath against her face. The slow, languish slide of a bead of sweat between her breasts. Lust burned, twisting in her body until it snapped. With the force of a cable breaking, a wave of intense white-hot pleasure hit her. Thrown into the maelstrom of her climax, she threw her head back and screamed. Every muscle rippled, clasped and relaxed spasmodically while stars danced on the back of her eyelids. Pleasure that bordered on pain cascaded over her like tidal waves.

The hot, searing wash of his ejaculate echoed through her. A startled gasp escaped her as she felt the pulse of his release, unfettered by the thin layer of latex that was normally used.

She trembled in his arms, her breathing unsteady as they sank to the carpet. Locked together, they leaned against each other and waited for the world to right itself.

Snuggled against him, Holly dozed. She nuzzled into his throat; the familiar smell of his aftershave and sweat were comforting. Absently, she trailed her fingers over his shoulders, tracing the hard pectoral muscles of his chest to tickle along his abdomen. She could feel the moist stickiness of his release within her and relished the notion that he'd lost complete control this time.

"Bed," Tyson whispered, and lifted her off him. He pressed a soft, warm kiss against her lips and stepped back. His arms were hard around her waist as he carried her to the bed and laid her down. A gentle kiss to her forehead and he straightened.

Holly wallowed in the warmth of the bed as she watched him walk through the shifting light of the candles and disappear into the bathroom. His taut, firm buttocks, marred by a couple of jagged scars, swung with each step. Regardless of the issues that plagued them, the sex had never cooled. If anything, it had gotten hotter as she'd let go of many of her inhibitions.

She stiffened slightly at the sound of running water even as she felt the warm stickiness that trickled from between her legs. The desire to tell him not to wash her was strong. A familiar ache awoke as she watched him walk toward her, face cloth in hand.

"Tyson," she started as he pushed the blankets aside. She reached for his wrists and stared into his eyes. "It's okay. You don't have to." The usual caring gesture seemed out of place, distant, and she wondered if it was because it meant more than something he did because he cared.

"Yes, I do," he replied with a grin. "You're probably sore. I should have been more careful," he explained as he wiped the milky fluid from her flesh.

His touch was gentle, caring, but Holly felt chilled to her very soul by it. Each swipe of the cloth took away another trace of their time together in this room. She smiled at him as he stood and tossed the soiled rag aside before he crawled in next to her.

"Night, love," he whispered, and pressed a small kiss on her bare shoulder.

"Good night," Holly whispered, her throat tight with emotion as she waited for him to want to come back to her for good. She lay silently, still, as he curled up behind her, his arm around her waist. The pain that ripped through her startled and confused her. She blinked at the burning behind her eyes, unmindful of the lone tear that tracked a path down her face.

From outside she could hear the sounds of the season—carolers singing, horse-drawn sleighs jingling—but it was distant. Like a memory all but forgotten. Holly turned to study Tyson who lay sleeping soundly, his face relaxed and clear of worry. Suddenly, anger as fierce as anything she'd ever known reared within her heart. She slipped from the bed and pulled on the fluffy white bathrobe that lay on the back of the chair. Curled up in it, she stared out the window.

Her mind raced with thoughts, with plans that had never reached fruition. Memories of the first year of their marriage played out in her mind, of the nights spent in pleasure. Right from day one, he'd taken care to use a condom. The few times they had been too caught up in the moment to use one, he'd washed her thoroughly. What had once been tenderness had become habit, a chore.

She didn't know why it hurt so much this time. Why the thought of him washing off the evidence of their mating should bruise her heart. It did, and that was enough. *How he must despise the thought of leaving me with that small bit of him. Oh, Tyson, why? What reason do you have for being so cautious, so careful? Can I live with so little from you?* She wondered as she studied him in the pale light of a streetlamp.

At thirty years old, Tyson Walker was a handsome man. His self-confidence and charisma made him stand out in a crowd. It was that very thing that had drawn her to him when they met. While it hadn't been an easy road, it had been one she walked proudly. Until now.

She rose and bent to retrieve his jeans. His wallet landed on the floor with a soft plop, and she picked it up. Tucked into the billfold was the familiar square package of a condom. Her trembling fingers pulled it free, and she stared at the brand, the color, as though seeing one for the first time. It was obviously from the supply that had come in her gift basket.

A sudden numbness settled into her bones. Holly sank into the overstuffed chair and wrapped her arms around herself. She turned to the window and stared out. The scene blurred and ran together as tears welled and spilled over. They had planned this getaway for months, from the time he'd come home after the accident. Everything, right down to the room, to the brand of condoms she'd requested in the basket, had been considered. Now she wondered why he was so determined to have this. Was this his way of softening her resolve, of easing her into the idea that he was going to stay on the circuit?

She knew she couldn't survive another year of broken bones and close calls. Of buckle bunnies tagging along after him, and doubts about herself, about his feelings. Of endless nights spent alone while he was off chasing some phantom. Her love was strong, but if she were brutally honest with herself, it wasn't so strong as to stand against the coming storm.

* * * *

Tyson shifted, a groan of protest at having to wake echoed in his ears. He blinked in the pale morning light as he reached across the bed for Holly. A soft sound drew his attention, and he rolled over to discover Holly dressed in worn denim and a flannel shirt at the window. He wondered what was so important beyond the glass that held her attention in the gray morning light, her arms crossed beneath her full breasts, a distant expression on her face in the reflection in the window.

"What time is it?" he croaked. Tyson pulled himself up to lean against the pillows, the sheet pooled at his waist.

"Eight-thirty," Holly replied, her tone flat, void of emotion as she stared out the window. Stiff, unyielding, she stood and turned away from him.

"What are you doing up? Why are you dressed?" He watched her when she turned to face him. A look of pain etched in her face, her eyes puffy and red, he knew she'd been crying. "Honey, what?"

"I'm going home," Holly declared. "I've got guests coming for New Year's Eve, Jack's bringing over that bay mare for me, and I've got a few items left to finish for that bridal party."

"Holly, we agreed to four days. What are you talking about?" Fear, heavy and stagnant, choked him. Its oppressive weight settled upon his chest like an elephant, and he shifted. He tossed back the blankets and got out of bed. Three strides and he stood before her, his hands rubbed her arms. "Holly, what's going on?"

"Seven."

"What?" Confused and uncertain, he gaped at her.

"We've been married for four years, Ty, and in that time we've made love seven times without a condom. I've been on the pill for three and a half years because you didn't feel ready for a family. Didn't matter, it still doesn't matter. You don't even want to touch me without one. Why can't you bring yourself to take me without one? Even this last time, it was so perfect—then you got up and rushed to clean away any sign of you on me. The sweat hadn't even dried on my skin and you were rushing to the bathroom. What's the matter, Ty, I'm good enough to screw but not good enough to leave your come in?"

"So I prefer to practice safe sex, what the hell does that have to do with this? With now?" Tyson demanded, anger rising to battle his fear as she turned from him, a distance, a coldness in her that he wasn't sure how to break through.

"I can't believe how foolish I've been." Holly brushed him aside. "You're always so careful not to leave any evidence of our activities. You wash up like a bloody surgeon afterward. You take your time, you erase any trace of your semen from my body like you're ashamed of me, of my being a sexual person." Bitterness saturated her voice as she held up the small foil packet. "You even carry a condom around with you. What happened last night, Ty? Get a little too carried away? Forget it was me you were fucking? Makes me wonder why a married man needs to have one of these on him at all times? It sure isn't because you're home with me all the time. I see you maybe a month out of the year. That's thirty nights of making love—no, not even that—of sex."

"Holly that isn't—"

"Isn't what?" Holly laughed, a cold disillusioned sound, before she bent to pick up her bags. "I've paid for the room for a week. Feel free to stay here, or go back to the circuit, or chase your buckle bunnies. I'm tired, Tyson. Tired of being your dirty little secret! I want you, I love you, but right now I don't like you. I need someone in my life that's going to be in my bed more than a few nights out of the year. You know, a husband, not just a lover who comes to me when it's convenient—or rather when he's so battered and broken that he can't chase that next eight second ride, or the next drunk tramp. I want to have a family, children, and you..." She sighed tiredly. "Well, you just want the rodeo."

"I see. This is about me not knowing what I want to do now, about the fact that part of who I am isn't there for me to fall back on. How childish and selfish, Holly. I've never..."

"No. This isn't about you." Holly shook her head, her eyes darting wildly. "This is about me. About wanting more than you're willing to give me. How long until I can have you in my life, my bed, for good? I'm tired of being lonely. I need more than just great sex," Holly whispered tearfully. "I married you, not the rodeo, not a ranch, but you. I don't want to spend the rest of my life waiting for you to decide you want me."

"Holly, don't do this. Not now," Tyson started, fear and anger broiling within his chest. The pain tore at him, ripping his defenses to shreds as he stared at the tears on her face.

"How can you stand there and say that? Of course I love you. I came home to you."

"Did you? Did you really come back to me, or did you slink back here because there's no expectation, no sense of urgency to be that next great rodeo star?" Holly shrugged. "Sometimes I wonder. We planned this trip so that we could get back what's been missing. The problem is—you don't believe there's anything missing. I thought I could pretend, that I could fix it, make things better. I was wrong. I'm sorry, Tyson, I really am."

Tyson gaped at her as she adjusted her coat and walked to the door. "Helluva Christmas present there, Holly," he croaked. His mind in a fog, he swallowed. He felt like he was in a box, everything distorted, muted shades of pain that swirled around him like snowflakes in the wind.

She stopped at the door; her body flinched as though struck. Pain etched in her face, worse than he'd ever seen before. Another tear streaked down her cheek. "I love you, Tyson, I'm just not sure that's what you want anymore. I'm not sure it's what I want anymore." She opened the door, picked up the bags on the floor, and stepped out.

Frozen in the middle of the room, Tyson stared at the door. An ache settled in his chest, and he blinked as he raked his hands through his hair. Desperately he turned, his gaze searching for something, anything. Silence was the only thing he found.

Chapter Five

Numb and unsettled, Holly stared at the tree in her living room. Her words to Tyson the day before echoed in her ears. He was probably still in Kamloops - he wouldn't come home until after the new year. Not when she'd ended their retreat the way she had.

"Merry fuckin' Christmas, Holly," she muttered to herself, and padded on sock feet into the kitchen. She stared at the kitchen table. Yards of materials rested on it in preparation for her sewing machine. The brilliant shades of silk drew an ache to her throat before she turned away.

Each bolt of fabric was for a specific order, a paying customer, yet she couldn't summon the desire to start.

Instead, she poured herself a cup of coffee and sat down to stare out the window. The blanket of snow that covered the pastures behind the house stretched out like her wedding train.

It was picture-perfect, just like her wedding day.

The carriage and white horses were missing, the guests, the music, but the magic still remained. If only she could go back. If she'd known then what she knew now, would she have been so happy? So blindly in love that she'd follow where he led?

The first two years they'd spent touring the circuit after the wedding had been perfect. Their happiness had carried from the nights to days. Tyson had been there, in body and in spirit. Now, even when his body was here, he wasn't, and she wondered what she could have done differently.

A sudden slam of a car door jarred her from her musings, and she turned to look at the clock. She wasn't expecting anyone. The mare she'd purchased for Tyson had been delivered, and her bed and breakfast guests were still days away. She rose and started for the front door. The door swung inward and a familiar figure stepped into the foyer, bringing a frigid blast of winter air.

Holly stared as Tyson closed the door and took his hat off. She watched him hang it on the peg. His coat followed, his boots kicked off, all without a word. "I wasn't expect you," she said, desperate for anything to break the silence, to hide the pain of her heart being ripped from her chest.

"I kinda figured that," Tyson drawled coldly. His long legs carried him past her. His arm brushed her shoulder, and she shivered slightly. Frozen, she listened to him make himself a cup of coffee.

Holly looked heavenward, her eyes burning with unshed tears. Please, let's just get through Christmas, she prayed, and turned to stalk into the kitchen. "What are you doing here? Thought you'd still be at the hotel."

Tyson leaned against the counter, his expression unreadable. His legs braced, arms crossed over his chest to make himself unapproachable. Grimness tightened his features, his lips pressed into a thin line. Anger darkened his blue eyes to slate, and the vein at his temple pulsed slightly.

"So what are you here for?" Sarcasm and anger dropped from each word. Holly gathered the bolts of fabric and the order forms in an attempt to keep busy. With him so close she wanted to forget her outburst, wanted to pretend again but couldn't. There were too many miles between them; they had grown in different directions. She'd chosen the life she wanted, rather than the one she struggled to survive with.

Her chest tightened and her throat closed as pain swelled. It rose to press in on her like a summer storm. She bit her lower lip to stem the flow of tears, to hide her emotions. A single tear escaped her control and she wiped at it furiously, aware of the cold gaze of her husband upon her.

"Anxious to get rid of me?"

Tyson's cold drawl was like a physical blow. She flinched at the tone, her hands resting on the bolt of fabric she had laid out on the shelf. Her head fell forward, and she closed her eyes. "I don't want to fight with you, Tyson." Her voice shook and a fine tremor raced through her body.

"No? Seems to me that is exactly what you want. You walked out on me, on our weekend, with a pretty little speech about me not being sure you're what I want. Now you're going to stand there and say you don't want to fight. You can't have it both ways, Holly. Life doesn't work that way!"

"What the hell do you know?" Holly faced him, her chest heaving with every breath. Pain stretched along the muscles around her heart as she glared at him. She clenched her fists to avoid throwing something. Instead, she stared angrily at him across the table. Perhaps it was best, like ripping off a band-aid. "How many times have you been home in the last year, Ty? Do you have any idea how many nights I've cried myself to sleep? How lonely I am? No, you don't. You follow your dreams, follow the call of the road, and leave me behind. I get a call here, a card there, periodically you stop in, we have a few hot nights in bed, and then you're gone again. What am I supposed to think?" Holly dragged her hands through her hair in agitation. "You call about as often as its convenient, which means less than twice a week if I'm lucky! I'm an afterthought in your life. The good little wife waiting at home while you're out partying with the sluts on the circuit, getting drunk with the boys. *Oh, wait, haven't talked to that albatross around my neck in a week, better phone her.*"

She paced back and forth across the kitchen, her heart pounding in her chest like a hammer. Rage, potent and venomous, oozed through her body, thickening her blood, pushing aside the pain for a few brief moments.

Her nostrils flared as she turned to face him. "You bought me a ranch, a house, livestock, but you never asked me if it was what I wanted. No, you just made the decision and then said adios." Ger hand closing around her half-filled coffee cup. As if in slow motion she watched it sail across the room to crash into the cupboard by his head. "I want my husband to want more than just a few hot nights between the sheets. What good is land or an empty house when you're off doing whatever or whoever you want? We did this weekend to keep our marriage alive, Ty. But if anything, it just showed me the truth. I want more than you can give me. I want you to need me, to love me more than some stupid rodeo. But you don't—do you? I was an idiot for thinking I could save something that's been dying a slow death. So do us both a favor and get the fuck out of my house. I don't imagine it should be too hard, Ty, just pretend you're running back to the circuit. Only don't bother coming back."

A hard shove sent a chair skittering across the floor as she stormed out of the room. Holly raced up the stairs, sobs of anger and misery exploded past her control. A dull roar echoed in her ears as she ran down the hallway.

The crash of the bedroom door was loud in the silence as Holly slammed it shut. She sank down to the floor, her sobs uncontrolled and bitter. "Damn you, damn you, damn you," she raged. "Oh God, why am I not enough?"

Curled on the floor, Holly cried desperately. She drew her legs up into a fetal position and closed her eyes. Each mouthful of air, each sob, was a physical ache. She felt his arms come around her and struggled against the falsehood of tenderness, of love from him.

"Damn you!" She pounded her fists against his chest angrily. "Why? Why am I not enough? Damn you to hell, Tyson Walker, I hate you! I hate you!"

"Shh," Tyson soothed. His hand cupped her head to his chest as he rocked her back and forth. "Shh, Holly, love. It'll be okay, it's going to be all right. I promise."

Holly shook her head, her sobs growing as she clung to his familiar warmth. Nothing would ever be right again, nothing. Her cries softened, her body relaxing into his embrace as the strain pulled her into exhaustion. Her fingers clutched at his shirt, even as she slid into a deep, troubled sleep.

* * * *

Tyson sat on the window seat, his eyes on Holly, who lay sleeping soundly. Her breath still hitched, her face streaked and mottled red from her crying. He turned his head and sighed. His worst fear had become reality. In giving Holly what he thought she deserved, he'd taken everything away from her. The house, the ranch, had been his attempt to give her the permanence and stability she'd always talked about in the early months of their marriage.

But it wasn't the kind of stability she wanted, what she needed from him. He was an idiot and the best thing in his life lay in tatters around his feet. Unless he could prove to her he was done. Prove he was home.

His heart contracted at the shuddery breath from the bed, and he shook his head. The circuit was not kind, it was hard and long. It broke men and women as easily as twigs in the wind. Destroyed lives, loves, it was a way of life that was empty. Barren compared to the warmth of his wife's arms.

He didn't know any other way. Tyson was rodeo. Could he handle the price if he continued as he had?

A seed of doubt had taken root in Holly's mind, doubt about his devotion, and his desires for her. It was something he had to fix. This was one demon he had to vanquish. Tyson slid off the seat and padded across the room to the bed. He leaned down and pressed a gentle kiss to her cheek.

What would the old man say right now? How would he handle the idea that his son had destroyed any chance for a future with a woman who'd loved him so much she'd waited years to have him? Ty shook his head. The old man would be furious, ranting and raving, ready to take his hide off. *You got a good woman, son. You do whatever it takes to make her happy.*

"I'm sorry, honey," he whispered softly, and pulled the blanket a bit higher over her. He turned and walked from their bedroom, his steps sure, confident. He hurried down the stairs and into the kitchen. He rifled through the drawers and cupboards until he came to the 'tryst' jar.

He pulled the stained-glass out and opened the lid. With a shaking hand, he reached into the jar and pulled out the roll of bills. A smile crossed his face as he tipped the porcelain horse up and emptied the loose and rolled coins onto the table. As he stared at the money, an idea formed in his head. One that would allow both of them to have what they wanted, what they needed. He reached for the phone and punched a familiar number into it.

"Hello?" Soft, aged, the feminine voice that drifted through the phone drew a smile from him.

"Hi Mom. Dad around?"

"He's watching the Finals."

Ty nodded, his stare fixed out the window. "Mom, I need help."

"What's wrong?"

"Holly…"

"Is she okay? What happened? Oh my goodness, I'll get your father. Just hang on a second." Fear tightened her voice.

"Mom, Mom, Holly's sleeping right now, safe and sound in our bed." Ty sighed. "We just hit – I don't know. I don't know how to explain it. But I hurt her bad and I need help."

"Let me get your father."

"Tyson Eldon Walker, what on earth is your mother going on about? Says you hurt Holly. If you laid--"

"I would never hit her, Dad. No, Dad, I want out." Ty rubbed at his face, the scratch of stubble loud in the kitchen. "I want...no, no, I need Holly."

"About damn time," his father drawled. "So what do you want to do about it?"

"I've got ten grand, and a ranch...what do you suggest?" Ty sank into the nearest chair, the butterflies in his belly settling. This was the right thing...the only thing he could do.

Twenty minutes later he hung up the phone, calm and at peace with his choice.

Above him the floor creaked and the tired shuffle of feet on the hardwood of the stairs drifted into the kitchen. He waited a moment for

Holly to come into the kitchen. When she didn't, he got up and walked to the doorway. She walked slowly, sadly, into the living room to sink into the overstuffed chair he loved.

Tyson leaned on the doorjamb and studied her carefully. Holly stared at the tree, her hands folded in her lap. Her shoulders were hunched as though a heavy weight rested upon them, and a sad look remained on her face.

"You know, it's not a good idea to cry yourself to sleep like that," Tyson drawled softly. He watched her flinch but she didn't move, didn't speak. "Holly?"

"What?"

Tyson exhaled sharply and strode over to kneel in front of her. "Darlin', look at me." He waited for her eyes to meet his, his hands clasped around her cold fingers. The exhausted, pain-filled look in her eyes ripped at his heart and tore at the scars he carried. He'd done this, hurt the one person he swore he would never hurt, and guilt clung tight to his throat. "You've got it all wrong."

She shrugged and shifted, a mulish expression on her face. "What have I got wrong?"

"When I said that I wasn't sure what I wanted to do now, I didn't mean I wanted to keep following the circuit." He paused. "Baby, rodeo's all I know. You know my background. You know how I grew up. I've never *not* been rodeo. I wish I could make you see what I want, but I can't. I don't want out of our marriage, I don't want to lose you."

Holly snorted with derision and looked away. "Sure you don't."

"Please, I don't want to lose us. I can't give you up. Try to understand, all my life I've been on the road."

"Tyson, I don't care anymore. I'm done. I've given and given and given – there isn't anything left." Holly pushed against him and started to get up only to sink back into the chair when he refused to move. "You know there is nothing about this that screams perfection. I want a marriage, a real one. One where my husband is home at night. One where when something happens I don't have to try to figure out time zones, is he at a rodeo function, is there someone with him. You don't. Let's leave it at that and forget about the rest. I won't risk you not being there for—"

"No, the woman I know, the woman I love, isn't a quitter. You're running scared for a reason." He shook his head. His gaze was steady as he studied her. Pride and anger danced with the pain in her eyes and beneath it—beneath it was something so sweet, so powerful he couldn't deny it. "And I want to know what that reason is."

Holly swallowed hard, a look of distrust mixed with fear crossing her features. He gave her a few moments to compose her thoughts, her words. Patiently, he waited, his eyes never leaving her face. With their future hanging in the balance, he had all the time in the world.

"Do you remember when you came home this last time? Way back in November, the night we spent out at the line shack?"

Tyson chuckled at her slight flush. It had been one of the hottest nights they'd ever shared. They had made love three times and not once had either of them worried about birth control. "Yeah, baby. I believe you told me the next day that you were too tired to breathe."

Holly shifted, and sucked in a deep breath. "I went to the doctor's office last week."

"And?"

The lone tear tracking down her face spoke volumes.

"Holly, what's going on?" Tyson shifted, fear overtaking any other emotion at the storm in her eyes. Whatever had happened was enough to terrify Holly. Dread filled him as he wondered if maybe he had somehow hurt her.

"I'm pregnant." A second tear tracked down her face. "You said so many times that you didn't want kids, that you weren't ready for them. It had been months since you were home and you always used a condom, so I figured what the hell. When it came time to get my prescription filled, I didn't. It's funny, I actually felt safe enough to go off birth control."

Tyson set back on his heels, his breath caught in his throat. "You mean to tell me that you're trying to get rid of me because of a baby?" he whispered, shock tightening his chest to a physical ache. The roaring in his ears echoed as he breathed softly for a few seconds, his eyes unyielding as he watched guilt settle in hers.

"I won't choose." She wrapped her arms around herself. "I can't."

Tyson chuckled and pulled her into his lap. "Dear God, woman, you scared the shit outta me. I didn't want kids while I was on the circuit, because I didn't want to miss anything with them. Oh, Holly, we're going to have a baby? You and me? For sure?"

"Doctor Hutchison says I'm about six weeks along. I know you think I've been drinking, but I haven't. The wine was a carbonated juice, even at the auction I wasn't drinking. I sat sipping on tonic water. I wanted one more memory of you before you left. I was greedy," she prattled, nerves and fear thickening her voice.

Tyson leaned forward, his lips crashing down on hers. He kissed her passionately, his tongue demanded entrance as he held her steady. The salt from her tears leaked through the kiss, mingling with the taste of coffee and Holly.

He cupped her face between his hands and forced her to look him in the eyes. "The most important thing in this world is my relationship with you. I gave you this house, this ranch, because you always said you wanted to put down roots. This isn't me trying to buy you. It's me trying to show you that I worship the ground you walk on."

Holly shook her head furiously, doubt lingering like a bruise on her pale skin. "But you're never home. I don't care about *things*, Ty, I just want you."

Ty nodded slowly, a pained, apologetic tone to his voice as he spoke softly. "That's true, I haven't been home too much. I've been riding the circuit. I know now I should have been there for you. I should have given you more than the crumbs I've expected you to be happy with. There's no way for me to undo the past, but I swear I will make it up to you. I'll do whatever you want, just please, please give us another chance."

Holly bit her lip uncertainly. "What about the baby?"

"I want the baby," Tyson whispered. "Admittedly, I'm terrified at the thought of being a dad, but I'm willing to try as long as it's with you. Please, don't throw us away."

The tears in her eyes slipped past her lashes to rain down her cheeks as she nodded and laughed. She threw her arms around his neck. "I promise I won't, Ty."

Ty crushed her to his chest and sighed. "You know, of course, that our tryst got interrupted by your rather impromptu display," he declared. "So I thought we could plan another one."

"Oh, Ty, we can't afford to. I mean, I've got work to do and without you working…" Holly started, only to frown as he covered her mouth with his hand.

The End

Trapped in a Blizzard

By Ireland Lorelei

Perla

It was a beautiful snowy day in January, and I was driving on a two-lane road in the middle of nowhere heading to a ski resort for a week getaway when my car broke down.

"What in the world," I said out loud as my car just stopped. "I know I have enough gas to get there, I just filled up the tank."

I try turning the key off and back on, but nothing, not even a sputter. "Great! Now what? I am about six miles from the resort and it's freezing outside," I said to myself. I check my cellphone and of course there is no service out here and the snow was picking up.

I get out of the car anyway, grab my suitcase and start walking through the snow pulling my luggage with me. I must have walked for two miles at least, when I saw a driveway, or I think it is. It's an opening in the trees at least. I decided to take a chance and walk a few fifty feet down that clearing in hopes of finding civilization. As I walked approximately thirty-six feet, I saw it, a cabin. There was smoke coming out the chimney which was scary that someone was there, but also a good thing that there is someone inside. It was also a blessing because I was cold and there is a working fireplace.

As I walked up to the door, I stood there for a minute or two trying to figure out if I should knock or not. *I mean, I am a woman all alone in the middle of no where.*

Before I could knock on the door, I hear a voice behind me.

"Good afternoon. Are you lost?" the voice said.

I turn around startled and came face to face with a man about 5'11" tall, completely bundled up so that I couldn't even make out his face and his hands were full of logs for the fireplace. Before I could speak, he continued.

"I am sorry. I didn't mean to startle you. My name is Troy Johnson and I own the cabin. I come up here a few times a year to decompress. I am a Police Officer from Detriot. What is your name and why are you walking through the woods in the middle of a snow storm?" he asked.

"First Officer Troy, I am freezing. Do you mind if we go inside?" I asked.

"I am sorry. Yes, let's go inside and get warmed up. I have some coffee on as well," he said as he opened the door still holding the firewood.

We walked in and immediately the warmth from the fire felt so good. He dropped the firewood by the fireplace and took off his coat and hat. *Wow! How lucky could a woman be if he really is a cop, because he is drop dead gorgeous. The muscles on his arms, could pick me up and fuck me in his arms while my back was up against the wall right here in the kitchen…or in the shower. Oh my, girl, get yourself together. Where did that thought come from?*

"So, your name? Where are you headed, and why are you walking around in the storm by yourself?" he asked again.

"Oh, I am sorry. I got caught up in the heat. My name is Perla Lettiere and I am from Highland Park. I was on my way to the ski resort a few miles up the road when my car just died. I have no idea what happened. I have no cell service, so my options were to walk the rest of the way to the resort and pray I made it before I froze to death or sit in my car and freeze to death. I choose to walk. I saw the opening in the trees and walked this way, praying it would leave me to somewhere to warm up and hopefully ride out this storm that seems to have come out of nowhere," I replied.

"Well, Perla, it is nice to meet you. My car is around back, but the roads are all closed now for the storm. We are in the middle of a blizzard. I guess you missed that on the weather report. I have a spare room and enough food and firewood for us both to make it a month without needing to eat sparingly. My badge and ID is on the kitchen counter. Feel free to look at it. The spare room is down that hall. The second door on the left. The first door on the left is the bathroom. Please feel free to make yourself at home. There is the one TV here in the living room, no phone, but there is internet. I try to disconnect as much as possible when I am here. I will add more wood to the fire and start us something to eat," he said.

"Thank you," I responded. "I will go drop my stuff in the spare room and then sit by the fire and warm up."

"I will have a cup of coffee or hot chocolate waiting on you. Which do you prefer?" he asked.

"Do you have marshmallows too?" I asked with a giggle.

"Actually, yes I do!" he said smiling.

That's when I noticed his dimples and almost tripped over my own feet! Damn he was so handsome.

"Hot chocolate it is then," I replied and grabbed by suitcases and headed down the hall. I needed to pull myself together!

Beth Freely, Carol Cassado, Ireland Lorelei, & Patricia

Troy

Wow! I am glad I got here yesterday! First I got here a head of the storm and second I am here to help her. I am glad that I didn't scare her to death though. She's such a petite woman. She shouldn't be out walking by herself in these woods. I can tell she is not one of those women who can take care of herself.

Hopefully she is not one of those needy or talkative women, and she keeps to herself. As much as I am that guy who will always help someone in need, I really need to continue to use this time to relax. It is the purpose I bought this cabin in Aspen so that I could take the month of December and half of January off from the force and decompress from all of the violence I see every day. I stock up enough groceries so that I only have to make one trip to town to get more groceries while I am here.

Tonight is my second night here and is the night I put up my Christmas decorations. I put up a tree in the living room, a few other inside decorations and a few lights around the porch. I guess I can ask her if she wants to help me. Christmas is my favorite holiday, like most people I guess.

She walks back into the kitchen.

"Here is your hot chocolate with marshmallows! I took out some chicken for dinner. I am going to decorate the house for Christmas in a little while. Do you want to help," I ask her.

"I would love to help you! You just tell me what you want where! And I will cook dinner. It is the least I can do for you rescuing me," she says.

"Thank you and I would never turn down a beautiful woman wanting to cook me dinner!" I reply.

We sit down at the table and just talked for at least an hour, getting to know each other.

Finally, I got up, and we grabbed the Christmas decorations out of the shed. Two hours later, we had all of the outside lights and decorations up. And I made us both some hot chocolate and put more wood on the fire for us to warm up before starting to decorate the Christmas Tree.

I turned on some Christmas music from my phone. We both sang along as we decorated the tree and the inside of the house. She hung some mistletoe from the ceiling right in front of the door on the inside and some as you stepped on the porch outside. She loves Christmas as much as I do.

Once we got everything up and all the lights turned on, she made dinner while I cut more wood.

After dinner, we sat in front of the fireplace.

"So, I have a story that my grandmother told me when I was a kid. She made it up, but would you like to hear it?" I asked.

"Yes, that sounds like a nice way to end the evening," she replies.

"Okay. The title is *Rudolph As Seen by Dasher,*" I say. *"Here goes! 'I remember the first time I saw Donner and Blitzen's new son, Rudolph. He could barely talk. His voice sounded funny, but other than that he looked just like the rest of us. He was one of Santa's reindeer. Every year Santa took myself, Dancer, Prancer, Vixen, Comet, Cupid, Donner and*

Blitzen up to guide his sleigh. We prepared for it all year. This year had been no different than any other. We tended to our families, taught the young to fly and other school educational courses that they would need. I was teaching a class one day and Rudolph sneezed. When he did, his nose turned to a bright red glowing light. Everyone immediately laughed when they noticed that he had been covering his nose up with black tar. It was the tar that had made his voice so funny, but nobody minded his voice. It was his nose that started all the laughs, jokes and the name-calling of the young Rudolph. From this day on, the kids would never let Rudolph join in any of the games or other activities. Several of the adults, went to Donner and Blitzen about their son. We teased them for having a son that was deformed. We really gave them a hard time. Santa saw him as unique and loved him very much. Rudolph was excited about Christmas Eve and had asked Santa if he could join the team and pull the sleigh this year, but Santa said that he needed to grow up. He was still a very young reindeer and pulling the sleigh was a hard job. Some overheard Santa's conversation with Rudolph, and they laughed and starting making fun of him even more. They told Rudolph that he would scare the children with his glowing red nose. But the night before Christmas, Christmas Eve this year, this is the day it all changed, for us all. I will never forget this night. It had been snowing hard all day. The powdery snow was thick on the ground and we were all excited. It is the biggest night of our lives. But once the snow started to stop falling, the fog was settling in. It was so thick that we couldn't see one foot in front of us. The sky was dark and the wind was howling. We had never experienced a fog like this. Donner, Vixon, and myself all went to Santa and asked him how would we fly tonight. Santa sounded optimistic and said, "we have time to wait it out. It will clearer up soon, I am sure." However, to himself, Santa was very worried. He didn't know if they would be able to deliver the gifts to all the good little boys and girls this year. After about an hour, Santa gathered his sleigh team and decided they would get an early start, that maybe they could still get all of the gifts delivered before it got any worse. As they started to take off, Santa couldn't see the road and the sleigh got stuck in the trees and even hit a few rocks. Santa then giving up said, "Christmas is cancelled this year. The children will be disappointed, but we can't see to fly tonight." They started back to the barn where the sleigh was kept and suddenly Santa remembered Rudolph with his bright shining nose. He realized at that moment that they could still make Christmas happen! Santa yells at the team, "Stay here. I will be right back!" He jumps off his sleigh and heads to Donner and Blitzen's house. He finds Rudolph asleep. He wakes him up and because Rudolph was excited to see Santa, his nose was glowing brighter than normal. Santa explains the weather and then says to Rudolph, "Rudolph with your nose so bright, won't you guide my sleigh tonight?" Rudolph jumps for joy and tells Santa that he would be honored. They head back to the sleigh and Santa hooks Rudolph up to the front of the team and they head out to deliver all of the gifts. Once back from delivering the gifts, Santa presented Rudolph with the Medal of Honor for his bravery. He was given a permanent spot on the team. The other reindeer never laughed or called him names anymore. The End!"

"Wow! That was interesting!" she said at the end! "I like it! I have one!"

"Thank you," I say. "Okay, I am all ears! Let's hear it!"

Perla

"Okay, It's called 'Mall Claus'," I told him. *"You would think that being Santa during Christmas at the mall would be a fun and exciting job, right? But not for this Saint Nick. Not by a long shot. Ethan Ford stood in a stall in the men's restroom outside of Dillard's in the Blackcreek Mall. He was trying to catch his breath and calm down while he made the 911 call. "911. What's your emergency?" the 911 operator asked. Whispering, Ethan replied, "There is an active shooter in the Blackcreek Mall." "Sir, I can barely hear you. Did you say you are at the Blackcreek Mall?" the operator asked. "Yes. There is an active shooter," Ethan replied again trying not to talk to loudly. Then the gunshots seemed to be getting closer and closer. Lots of shots. Then he realized the 911 operator had been speaking to him. "I am sorry. What did you say? The gunshots are getting louder. They must be getting closer," Ethan said into the phone a little louder than before to make sure she heard him. "Okay, Sir. I think I understand. You are in the Blackcreek Mall and there is gunshots going off. Correct?" asked the operator. "Yes, that is correct. I am the Santa from the middle of the mall. When I heard the first shots, I ran in the opposite direction of where they were being fired. I ran towards Dillard's and down the hall to the restrooms. I am in a stall now. People were scattering and running everywhere. As I was running, I could hear screams coming from behind me and more shooting. I don't know what is going on," Ethan said in a panic. "Okay, calm down. Is there anything you can tell me about how many gunmen, or how many are injured? What about what stores it seemed like the gunmen are in?" the operator asked. "I honestly don't know. I can tell you that the shots seem to be louder now near where I am," he replied. "Okay. Stay calm. Tell me your name. Mine is Sherri," the operator said. "Hi Sherri. My name is Ethan. Ethan Clark," Ethan replied. "Hello Ethan. I have officers and the paramedics on the way. Stay calm, stay hidden. Do not go out of the bathroom for any reason until one of the officers comes in to get you. They will announce who they are and ask for you by name, okay? That way you know it is safe to come out," Sherri told him in a reassuring voice. "Thank you, Sherri. Please don't hang up, okay. I don't think I can make it through this without you," Ethan said. "I promise you I will be right here with you until the officers come and get you," Sherry responded. As Ethan sat and waited on the officers to come and get him, he started to hear more commotion. There were more gunshots going off. "Sherry, are you there?" Ethan asked. "Yes, I am still here," Sherri replied. "I hear more gunshots," Ethan stated. "It's okay. The police just got there and SWAT is making an entrance through several of the mall main and side doors as we speak. You may hear a lot of things going on, but remember, no matter what, you stay right where you are," Sherri told him. "I will," Ethan said. About fifteen minutes later, Ethan hears the door to the restroom open. "Ethan Clark, this is Officer Justin Green. Are you still in here?" Ethan walks out from the stall and says, "Yes, I am still here." The officer asks to speak to the 911 operator, "Ma'am this is Officer Green. I have Mr. Clark." As Ethan and the officer head out, Ethan sees blood everywhere and bodies still on the floor. At nineteen years old, he decided at that moment that he would never play Santa again in any mall. The End!"*

"I have to say that was a very interesting Christmas story!" He laughed.

"Well, I thought so too! I just made it up as I went!" I say laughing so hard I thought I was going to ball up.

Troy

For the next four days, we stayed shut up in that cabin. I would take care of the fire and we would split the cooking. On the evening of the fourth night, our relationship started to change. Every night we would either sit and talk, watch Christmas stories on the TV, or tell Christmas stories.

This afternoon we decided to go for a short walk through the backyard to see the sunset over the mountains.

"This is gorgeous. I am so glad we decided to do this. The colors of pink and orange are breathtaking hitting the snow on top of the mountain," she says as the sun starts to come down close to the mountains.

I am too busy looking at her. The way her eyes glow when she is happy is what takes my breath away. But I tell her, "Yes, it is a beautiful site." Meaning her and not the sunset.

When we got back to the front porch, it was slippery, and she slipped into my arms, right under the mistletoe. We both looked up and then at each other. She smiled and I looked deep into her eyes.

There is no question that I think she is beautiful and sexy as hell. I am also starting to have feelings for her. So, it is easy to lean down and kiss her. I have wanted to nipple on her lips for days. But the peck wasn't doing the job. I wanted more. I spread her lips with my tongue and she let me in and wrapped her arms around my neck. It was as if time stood still. I have no idea how long we stood there. When I broke off the kiss, I kept my arm around her waist as we walked into the cabin.

"Thank you for catching me! That could have been very embarrassing if I would have fallen on my ass!" she says as I shut the door behind us.

"I would have never laughed if you had fallen, but I am glad I was there to catch you," I tell her.

She gives me the biggest smile and says, "I am going to start dinner. Do you want some hot chocolate while you wait for it to be done?"

"Yes, I would love some and after we eat, I have another story for you," I told her.

"I can't wait," she says.

After dinner, we sit down in front of the fireplace and I tell her the story of the "Elf Pink Slip". *"It is almost that time! The countdown for Christmas is around the corner! As Santa's helpers are working their magic on the assembly lines making sure that every good little boy and girl gets what is on their Christmas list, something unusual happens.*

All of a sudden the line stops! The belt on the toy drop came out a complete halt and everyone stopped moving. In comes Starmie from her break. "Gather around everyone. I just heard some news that we are all going to want to hear," Starmie said as she walked through the center of the floor yelling from right to left to make sure everyone heard her. The assembly line completely stopped from the elf's that were wrapping the presents and marking them off the list, to the elf's putting the toys on the belts, all the way down to the elf's that were taking the gifts off the belts and passing them from one to another until they reached the bag that was to go on the Santa's slay. Everyone starts whispering among themselves, "What is going on?" "Why is she stopping us?" "What is she talking about?" When everyone had gathered around, she said,

"Okay everyone, quiet it down so I can tell you what I just heard in the break room." Everyone got quiet. "Okay, so I was sitting in the break room and outside in the hallway I heard Santa and Melo (the head elf) talking. They said that one of us is getting fired today," Starmie said. It was as if everyone was talking at the same time. There was just a loud echo that she was sure everyone in the building was going to come running in to see what was going on, especially Santa. Starmie didn't want anyone in management to know that not only did she overhear them, but that she told everyone. Now all of the elf's were on edge. Maybe she had done the wrong thing. Maybe she shouldn't have said anything, especially without knowing 'who' they were letting go. Starmie's friends, Joyful, Precious, and Muffin, all ran over to her asking did she hear anything else, did she know who it was, or did they give any hints. She told them no. She had no idea or even a guess as to who it was. For the rest of the day, everyone was nervous. They did go back to work, but it took a while for everyone to calm down long enough to get back to work. Now they were all behind on their duties and wouldn't make their production

numbers. But they were all in overdrive to try and make them anyway. At five minutes to 5 pm, Santa and Melo came in. Melo yells, "Everyone gather around. Santa has something he would like to say." Starmie thought to herself that this couldn't be about who they were letting go. Santa would never fire someone in front of the whole crew. Would he? "Hello my little elf's!" Santa said. "As you all know it is about time for Christmas. We have four more days until we get to make all the dreams come true for the good little boys and girls this year. You have all worked so hard this year, just like every year. But this year I wanted to do something a little different. I wanted to start picking one of you, who has done the best work all year long, to come join me on my slay on Christmas Eve!" You could tell that everyone was in shock. All mouths dropped open. Starmie was shocked the most. She had misunderstood the conversation she overheard. Santa was firing someone, he was letting someone go with him. "And this years winner is……….Decorata! Congratulations!" Santa yelled. The End!"

"Okay, that was good!" She giggled.

"Why, thank you madam!" I say as I stand up. I wanted to kiss her again, but I didn't want to be pushy. "Well, good night! I will see you in the morning for breakfast."

"Good night, Troy," she says as she stands up and faces me. She plants a kiss on my cheek and walks away.

Wow, am I missing the signs? Does she want me as much as I want her? Should I follow her down the hall? Should I make a move tonight, or maybe tomorrow night, or maybe I am misreading her and I shouldn't do or even say anything.

Perla

Well I really thought he may take the hint, but I guess not. He didn't follow me. Could it be that he doesn't want me? Maybe he just doesn't find me attractive.

Perla

When I wake up in the morning, it smells like coffee and bacon. It smells delicious, so delicious that my stomach growls! I rush into the bathroom, brush my teeth and my hair. I didn't even bother to get dressed. I threw on my robe and headed towards the kitchen. *This is one way to tell if he feels for me what I feel for him, desire.*

"Good morning! The smell of coffee and bacon were filling up my room! I didn't realize I was so hungry until I smelled the food!" I say to him.

When he turns to look at me with a plate of food in his hand, I see automatically the affect seeing me in my robe does to him. He almost drops the plate before he gains his composure and says, "Um…yes. I fixed bacon, eggs, grits, biscuits and of course coffee."

"Thank you," I say as he sets the plate down on the table where I sit. I make my coffee as he makes him a plate.

We set in silence while we ate. I cleared the table and the dishes when we were done and he went to grab more wood for the fire.

Then we go sit on the couch to watch TV when he put his arm around my neck. I looked up at him, and then he leaned down and kissed me. At first it was just a soft light kiss, but it turned into him forcing my mouth open with his tongue.

After a few minutes we headed to his bedroom. He took off my clothes first and then his own. He laid over me and spread my legs. He started biting and pulling on my nipples one right after the other making her release little screams of ecstasy all while sliding one then two fingers inside of my core. Then he started licking and penetrating with his tongue until I came undone.

But I still wanted more. I wanted him inside of me. I wanted to feel every inch of him until it felt like I was choking on him. I begged for him to give me more, to fill me up.

He turned me around so that I was laying on my stomach and told me to put my arms above my head. He slipped something over my eyes, then I felt him grab my right arm and something went around my wrist and my whole arm pulled to the right. I heard a snap and I went I tried to move it, I couldn't. He grabbed my left arm and I said, "What are you doing?"

"I promise you that you will enjoy it. I am not going to hurt you. I am going to pleasure your body like you have never had it pleasured before," he replied as he did the same to my left arm that he did to my right.

I didn't know what to say, but I knew he was making me feel so good. He pushed me legs apart and then pushed me up on my knees. I felt something cold being rubbed on my butt cheeks, and then I felt an invasion. At first it hurt, but whatever it was he was easing it in. I wasn't sure if it was his penis or not. Then I felt him go inside my kitty cat, but the other invasion was still there. I couldn't take it, the penetrations into both was so much. Not painful, but so intensifying and amazing. I was coming undone again, over and over again. I had never felt so much pleasure before.

The harder he pounded, the more intense the sensations got until he finally came inside me. When he pulled out, he then pulled out the toy from my butt. He slide my legs down and unhooked my arms. Then he rolled me over onto my back and took off the blindfold. He wrapped me in his arms and asked, "How was it? How do you feel?"

My reply surprised myself. When he had started hooking my arms and especially the intrusion into my butt, but I told him, "I have never felt better and so satisfied."

My whole life changed when my car broke down that afternoon on my way to the ski resort. I found love and sexual desires that I never knew I had.

Troy

I never would have thought when I came to the cabin for my annual Christmas trip that I would get the best Christmas present ever, one that money could never buy. What started with me trying to help a lady who got stuck in a blizzard, ending up becoming the love of my life. If it hadn't been for the mistletoe though, I never would have acted on the feelings I had growing for her. It just goes to show that Christmastime is truly the most magical time of the year.

The End

Made in the USA
Columbia, SC
23 December 2022